She Was Face to Face with Destiny.

His eyes openly raked her body and she felt a heated flush rise through her.

"Are you quite through? Do I meet with your approval? If not, I'll be only too happy to leave."

Cory smiled arrogantly. "Why would I want you to leave? You're a most intriguing woman. First you appear to be a withered old maid, then yesterday, at your apartment, you looked quite the femme fatale. And now you appear to be every inch the handsomely efficient young businesswoman. You have definite possibilities, Miss Lorrimer. You may be quite an asset to the company—and to me."

JOANNA SCOTT
is a former teacher who gave up that career to follow her dream: writing. She has traveled widely, researching her novels, but is especially fond of California, the state that she and her husband of twenty-three years call home.

Dear Reader:

Silhouette Books is pleased to announce the creation of a new line of contemporary romances—*Silhouette Special Editions*. Each month we'll bring you six new love stories written by the best of today's authors— Janet Dailey, Brooke Hastings, Laura Hardy, Sondra Stanford, Linda Shaw, Patti Beckman, and many others.

Silhouette Special Editions are written with American women in mind; they are for readers who want more: more story, more details and descriptions, more realism, and more *romance*. *Special Editions* are longer than most contemporary romances allowing for a closer look at the relationship between hero and heroine with emphasis on heightened romantic tension and greater sensuous and sensual detail. If you want more from a romance, be sure to look for *Silhouette Special Editions* on sale this February wherever you buy books.

We welcome any suggestions or comments, and I invite you to write us at the address below.

Karen Solem
Editor-in-Chief
Silhouette Books
P.O. Box 769
New York, N. Y. 10019

JOANNA SCOTT
Manhattan Masquerade

Silhouette Romance

Published by Silhouette Books New York

America's Publisher of Contemporary Romance

Other Silhouette Romances by Joanna Scott

Dusky Rose
The Marriage Bargain

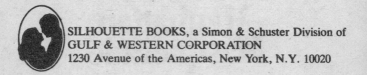

SILHOUETTE BOOKS, a Simon & Schuster Division of
GULF & WESTERN CORPORATION
1230 Avenue of the Americas, New York, N.Y. 10020

Distributed by Pocket Books

ISBN: 0-671-57117-6

First Silhouette Books printing November, 1981

10 9 8 7 6 5 4 3 2 1

All of the characters in this book are fictitious. Any resem-
blance to actual persons, living or dead, is purely coincidental.

Map by Tony Ferrara

America's Publisher of Contemporary Romance

Printed in the U.S.A.

To my mother and my mother-in-law

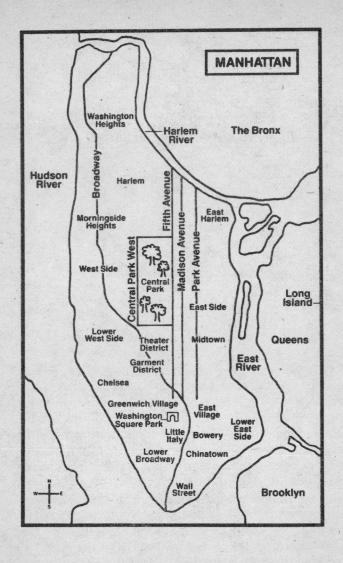

Chapter One

Samantha Lorrimer stormed to her desk and began opening the drawers, emptying them, then closing them with a furious bang. After removing all her personal belongings from the desk drawers and sliding them into a large brown envelope, she stalked out of the office, slamming the door behind her, then walked to the elevator and began pressing the down button repeatedly, as if to hasten its arrival. The outer doors had barely opened when she charged through them, startling the young elevator operator, who turned and looked at her quizzically.

"Is something wrong, Miss Lorrimer? You don't usually leave work so early in the day."

"I've just quit my job, Tommy," Samantha

said as they rode down to the lobby. "I guess I won't be seeing you anymore."

The elevator stopped at the main floor lobby and Samantha exited, waving good-bye to Tommy.

"Good luck, Miss Lorrimer. Stop by and say hello if you're ever in the neighborhood."

Samantha spun quickly through the revolving doors into the skyscraper-shaded sunshine of Wall Street. The New York City financial district was all but deserted at this hour of the day, since no one dared take a break from work until the stock market closed at four o'clock. Then the representatives and their secretaries could be seen heading for their favorite cocktail lounges to make up for the dry sandwiches they had eaten at their desks.

Well, thought Samantha, there'll be no leisurely lunch hour for me until I land another job. She wondered how difficult it would be to secure new employment, considering she could hardly expect a good reference from Mr. Cahill. He hadn't exactly been civil to her after she pushed his hands off her waist and slapped him full in the face. Why was it that every paunchy executive in his mid-fifties considered himself a Lothario when it came to his secretary? Well, she was not about to be pawed by those lecherous old men even if it meant she had to change jobs every other day.

Swinging her head petulantly, she caught a glimpse of her reflection in an adjacent store window. Her long blond hair was parted in the center and fell to her shoulders in a sleek, velvety cascade. Bright blue eyes flashed impishly above a small straight nose where a feathery sprinkling of freckles highlighted a honey-smooth complexion. She was a tall girl and she emphasized her height by wearing high-heeled spectator pumps. Despite her height, she appeared fragile because her delicate bone structure gave her the regal profile of a finely carved Greek goddess.

It's just not right, she thought, looking away from the window and continuing down the street. I don't do anything to encourage their advances, so why do they all consider me fair game? I'm just an ordinary small-town girl, certainly not a femme fatale. Why can't they leave me alone and let me do my work?

She was so angry she was practically talking to herself and scarcely watched where she was walking, which resulted in her charging wildly into the powerful chest of an unsuspecting man walking in the opposite direction. His arms circled her protectively and the shocked look on his sun-tanned face gave way to one of indulgent amusement as Samantha's startled face met his smiling gray eyes. She tried to step away but his arms tightened around her, drawing her back toward him.

"Not so fast," he said teasingly. "We've barely gotten acquainted."

Samantha shook herself free and studied the coolly composed man who continued to block her path. His carefully styled dark brown hair met the collar of his white silk shirt, which contrasted attractively with his hand-tailored charcoal-gray suit. He was at least a head taller than she was, and, although he wore the attire of an executive, Samantha thought that his muscular arms and chest would be equally at home on the athletic field.

"I'm sorry; it was all my fault. I wasn't looking where I was going," she said in embarrassment and began to move away.

His hand came out to restrain her. "Wait a minute. You're not just going to dash off like that, are you? At least let me buy you a cup of coffee."

Samantha looked at him and shook her head. "No thanks. I have to be going," and she strode away, leaving him to stare in bewilderment at her retreating back. The last thing she wanted now was masculine companionship.

She was still steaming when she reached the small brownstone in Greenwich Village where she shared an apartment with a girlfriend. She opened the door and let herself in, tossing her envelope onto the sofa and slumping down beside it.

"Sam . . . is that you?" said the tall, dark-haired girl who came walking into the room. "What are you doing home this early?" She glanced at the brown envelope lying next to Samantha. "Oh, no, don't tell me you've quit another job. Or have you been fired this time?"

"Well, Janet," said Samantha, kicking off her shoes and stretching her long, slender legs along the edge of the sofa, "you might say I refused to perform certain duties and was relieved of the ones I thought I was hired to do."

Janet raised her eyebrows disbelievingly. "You mean old man Cahill made a pass at you? He's old enough to be your father, or even your grandfather. The theater seems like good clean fun in comparison to what takes place in the world of high finance."

"It's more like the world of high jinks," said Samantha, closing her eyes and resting her head against the back of the sofa. "You know I only want to do my job and receive a decent salary for it. We took this apartment together, and you won't be able to keep it if I can't pay my half. And I'll never be able to do that if I keep losing jobs. Why can't any of these men understand that? I'm just not interested in having an affair. You know I'm not that sort of girl, Janet."

Janet gracefully raised a slender hand to the nape of her neck and fanned the shimmering fall of ebony hair falling about her shoulders. "I know, among my friends you're known as Little Miss Icicle. But you have to admit, you just don't have the proper physical contours for an icicle. With your face and figure you should try to get some modeling jobs. If you have to submit to an employer's advances, you might as well be paid a decent wage for your services."

Samantha shook her head. "Come on, Janet, I'm nowhere near attractive enough to compete with you for modeling jobs. Besides, I came to New York to make a career for myself; I just didn't realize I would be expected to perform a wide range of extracurricular activities in order to keep a job. I really want to learn the stock market; I just wish there was some way to make men disregard my anatomy and judge me by my mind."

. Janet lit a cigarette and cast a long searching look at Samantha. "There might be a way, but it would be a terrible waste."

Samantha swept her feet to the carpet and stared at Janet. "You think you know of a way I can keep a job without getting pawed by some lecherous old man?"

"Well, I don't know. It's so way out that it's ridiculous. But it just might work."

"Tell me! I'll try anything short of murder, and there have been times when I've even considered that. Come on, let me hear your idea. Don't keep me in suspense. I'm desperate."

"Do you remember the part I had in my very first play? You know which one I mean . . . at the Cherry Lane Theater."

Samantha thought for a moment. "Yes, I remember. You played the part of a little old lady, selling apples in the Bowery. It was called *The Street of Broken Dreams*, wasn't it? But what's that got to do with me?"

"Sam, think for a minute, will you? Look at me. Do you remember how I looked when I played the apple lady? I was still the same me, but the stage makeup worked wonders. Your entire problem stems from your naturally seductive appearance. You don't do anything to encourage it . . . you were just born with it. But you haven't tried disguising your appearance and making yourself less attractive. That's what I had in mind. I think it's insane and a terrible waste, but if that's what you want . . . why not?

I can show you how to apply stage makeup to add wrinkles and bumps to your face. Then, with the right hairdo and different clothes, I think we can make you downright unattractive."

Samantha sat forward in her seat. "Do you really think we can do it, Janet? Are you sure? I mean, will I be able to carry the whole thing off on a long-term basis?"

Janet stubbed out her cigarette and smiled. "Yes, I'm sure we can do it. In fact, I think it might be fun . . . fooling all those lecherous old men. But are you sure you want to do it? Remember, there won't be any young men asking you for dates."

"That's just fine with me. Their ideas are no different from the older men's. They just have less money and more energy. As far as I'm concerned, I'd like to declare all men off limits. When can we begin?"

Janet got up from her chair. "Why not right now?" She walked toward the bedroom.

Samantha followed and watched as she took out her makeup case. Then she sat down in the chair Janet indicated. Janet removed some small pots of makeup from the case and flipped on the circle of bright lights surrounding the dressing-table mirror. She swept Samantha's hair back from her face with a large chiffon bandanna.

"Let's see," she said. "First off, that nose is a bit too pert and perfect for a businesslike old spinster. Why don't we just add this little putty bump? There, that ruins a perfectly good nose.

Now I'll just add some wrinkles on your cheeks and under your eyes. Then we'll cover the entire mess with some gray-tinged pancake makeup and *voilà*, you're not so pretty anymore."

Obviously enjoying her work, she took Samantha's long flaxen hair and twined it into a tight little bun at the nape of her neck. The silver-blond mane, which had seemed so thick and luxurious when it hung free, now took on a dull, ashen appearance. After adding a pair of clear-lensed, horn-rimmed glasses she stood back to inspect her handiwork. "Well, what do you think? Doesn't stage makeup work wonders?"

Samantha couldn't believe her eyes. "I'll say it does. I don't even recognize myself. I'm not sure anyone will hire me, looking like this. But if I *do* land a job, I'm quite certain the boss won't make a pass at me."

"Wait a minute," Janet said. "Not so fast. We still have the problem of a very curvaceous body to contend with." She eyed the clinging jersey blouse with its enticingly feminine vee neck and grimaced as she saw the long slender legs peeping below the flares of a softly pleated linen skirt. "Those clothes will have to go. Come on . . . take off the makeup. We've got some shopping to do and I know just the place to do it."

Samantha winced a little while later as they entered a store that catered to older women with more mature, heavy-set figures. Janet helped her select several severe, high-necked white blouses and somber, shapeless suits in shades of brown, blue, and olive green. She completed the picture with several heavy pairs of dull beige cotton stockings and some low-heeled sensible shoes.

Samantha couldn't believe the reflection staring back at her from the mirror. "Janet, no man will even think of making a pass at me now. I look totally undesirable. How can I ever thank you enough?"

Samantha spent Sunday checking the want ads and circling the interesting ones. Bright and early Monday morning, she donned her disguise and started applying for the advertised jobs. The one that interested her most had been placed by Cory Talbott Associates, one of the most respected investment brokerage houses in the city. Samantha was sure she could learn a lot by working with such a prominent firm. In fact, given the right opportunities, she might even be able to find advancement within the company itself.

Talbott Associates occupied the entire top floor of a magnificent skyscraper. Samantha took a deep breath, straightened her shoulders and strode defiantly through the gold-lettered glass doors. The receptionist eyed her quizzically.

"May I help you?"

"Yes. I'm interested in applying for the secretarial job advertised in yesterday's paper."

The girl reached into her desk drawer and handed Samantha a printed form. "Please complete this application and return it to me. You may use that desk," she said, pointing to a small desk near the entrance.

Samantha began to fill in the application form. Most of the questions were easy for her to answer. She was happy that federal employment laws forbade asking questions about age on job applications. She didn't want to tell any outright lies, and answering that question truthfully might present some problems. After finishing the application, she returned it to the receptionist, who placed it at the side of her desk.

Samantha knew that her typing and steno were well above average, but she was still relieved after she had been tested in both and done well.

The receptionist seemed pleased as well and led Samantha into a large private office. The gray-haired woman seated behind the French provincial desk looked up and motioned Samantha toward a seat at the side of the desk. The woman wore a beautifully tailored and obviously expensive blue suit. It was conservative, but stylish, and Samantha felt extremely uncomfortable in her stage makeup and dowdy clothing.

"I see you have superior secretarial skills, Miss Lorrimer; however, you list no references. Surely a woman of your age must have some previous employment experience."

"I spent most of my adult years caring for a sickly relative," Samantha lied reluctantly. "She's gone now and I need a job."

The woman, who had introduced herself as

Mrs. Harrison, frowned. "You're not quite what we expected, but I think you may be just the person we've been looking for. As you may know, Talbott Associates is a very respected firm, with offices in most of the world's major cities. Although the company is called Talbott Associates, it is actually run by one man, Cory Talbott. For many years, I was Mr. Talbott's secretary. However, recently the company's business has become so complex that my function has become more like that of an office manager. I no longer seem to have enough time to adequately perform my secretarial duties. Mr. Talbott needs someone to handle his personal correspondence and business affairs, and I simply cannot give him the time he needs. We've had several girls from our secretarial pool attempt to fill the position. This is our normal procedure for a job at this level; however, they were all young and apparently desired something more than a business relationship with Mr. Talbott. Mr. Talbott, however, never mixes his personal life with the business of this office. You seem to be a settled, level-headed person, and I'm sure you would have no similar failing. However, the final decision must be Mr. Talbott's. I'll see if he's free to interview you now. Please excuse me, Miss Lorrimer."

Samantha could hardly believe her ears. Imagine working for a man who wanted nothing but a strictly business relationship, a man with a reputation like Cory Talbott's, a man known as the Wizard of Wall Street. Samantha was sure she could learn more about the business world from him than she could in any night-school course.

Moments later, Samantha followed Mrs. Harrison into a huge paneled office. The entire back wall was windowed and afforded a breathtaking view of the New York harbor. All the furniture in the room was of oiled teak. Although massive in size, the furniture's simple lines bespoke classic elegance. However, the dimensions of the furniture seemed insignificant in comparison to the dynamic energy emanating from the man who stood behind the desk holding his hand out to Samantha. His sun-tanned face contrasted with his bright white silk shirt and his dark gray worsted suit rippled with the muscles coursing beneath it. But it was his piercing eyes that drew Samantha's attention and held her spellbound, for she was staring into the face of the man she had collided with on Wall Street just two days before. She gulped nervously, certain that if anyone could discover her disguise, Cory Talbott would. But although his eyes searched her face inquisitively, he gave no sign of recognition and continued to behave as if he were seeing her for the first time. His deep, commanding voice brought Samantha back to reality.

"Sit down, Miss Lorrimer. Mrs. Harrison has spoken most enthusiastically of you. No doubt she has also told you of my desperate need for a private secretary. The job is rewarding, but difficult. There are no set hours and when we're involved in an important transaction we often work into the small hours of the morning. I hope you can commit yourself to such a program when the need arises."

Samantha nodded her head. "I'm completely without ties. I'll be available whenever I'm needed."

Cory Talbott flashed a wide grin. "Mrs. Harrison, I believe we've found the right person for the job." He looked back at Samantha. "I trust you know about the wages and other working conditions." He noted Samantha's acquiescent nod. "Very well, then, it's all settled. When can you start?"

"Right now, if you'd like. I have no other commitments for the remainder of the day."

"Excellent!" he said with undisguised enthusiasm. "Mrs. Harrison will show you to your desk. I'll be calling on your services shortly."

Samantha followed Mrs. Harrison to the secretarial desk just outside Talbott's private office and listened attentively while she explained the various machines and paperwork. In a short while the intercom buzzed, and Samantha, taking her steno pad and pencils, went into the private office.

Cory Talbott was leaning back in the large black leather chair behind the desk, his aquiline profile handsomely silhouetted against the early-afternoon sun. At the sound of the door closing, he swiveled his chair and faced Samantha. "I have some letters I'd like to dictate. Have a seat."

He began dictating as soon as she sat down, and he spoke rapidly, pausing only long enough to gather his thoughts for the next sentence.

Within an hour, he had dictated seven letters. "Do you think you can get those out this afternoon?"

Samantha closed her pad. "I won't leave until they're done, and I'll make certain they get to the mailroom before I leave this evening. Will there be anything else?"

Talbott leaned comfortably back. "No, that will be all. Thank you, Miss Lorrimer."

He smiled, and she found herself blushing. Strange icy fingers began walking up her spine and she almost fled from the room.

Obviously, something was wrong with her. Well, whatever it was, she had better make a quick recovery. She could just imagine Cory Talbott's reaction if he ever learned that the staid Miss Lorrimer had palpitations every time he smiled at her. Forget it, she told herself harshly. This job is too important to risk by developing a crush on the boss.

Samantha was typing the last letter when a small delicate blonde opened the office door. She was dressed in an exquisite confection of frothy pink, and her shapely legs were beautifully shown off beneath the swirling hem of the light chiffon skirt. She tilted her head at Samantha. "You must be Cory's new secretary. How nice . . . you look so comfortably reliable. I'm Denise Gerard, Cory's fiancée. I'll just walk on in. He's expecting me."

Samantha rose quickly from her desk, blocking Denise's entry. "Please, Miss Gerard. I've been instructed to announce all visitors before they enter. Why don't you just wait here while I buzz him? It will only take a minute."

Denise's eyes blazed with anger as she waited for Samantha to announce her presence. In a few seconds, Cory Talbott came sauntering through the door, a relaxed smile playing about the corners of his mouth. He leaned against the door jamb, watching Denise drum her fingers impatiently on Samantha's desk.

"Miss Lorrimer, I *am* impressed. No other secretary has ever been able to announce Miss Gerard's presence. She usually just barges in and interrupts whatever I'm doing."

Denise turned and looked up into Cory's eyes. She walked toward him and placed her arms around his neck. "Ah, but, darling, you seem to enjoy my interruptions so much. I've never heard you complain before. Come on, let's go inside so I can greet you properly." A moment later the door had closed behind them.

For some inexplicable reason, Samantha was terribly annoyed. She felt horribly unattractive in her drab brown clothing, but she had wanted to look unattractive. How then could she explain her sudden desire to be wearing a more appealing outfit? It just didn't make any sense. She supposed it was because she wasn't used to her new image. It would probably take time to adjust to it. Still, she had this wild urge to change into her sexiest outfit, go into Cory's office, and make him look at her the way he had just looked at Denise Gerard. Shaking her head to clear it, she reminded herself that she was here to work;

even contemplating such ridiculous behavior could make her lose what looked to be the best job she ever had.

In a short while, Cory and Denise came out of the office. He had his arm around her waist and she was clinging to him in a kittenish manner. Cory stopped by Samantha's desk. "I'll be leaving for the day. Just finish what you're working on and then you may leave. Check with Mrs. Harrison if you have any questions."

Samantha left the building less than an hour later and walked toward the corner bus stop. Although it was a pleasant evening, she felt tired and was eager to get home so she could relax. Janet was waiting for her on the sofa when she let herself into the apartment. She eyed Samantha curiously.

"Well, tell me what happened. Did you get a job? How did things go?" She followed Samantha into the bedroom. "Are you going to tell me what happened or let me burst from curiosity?"

Samantha began changing out of her clothes. "I got a fantastic job with Talbott Associates. I'm private secretary to Cory Talbott, president of the firm. Now hear this, I landed the job because of my appearance. The other girls they tried to promote from within the company were too flighty for the position. Can you believe such luck? I don't know how I'll ever be able to thank you enough, Janet. This is probably the best thing that has ever happened to me."

Janet laughed. "Sam, you are one crazy lady, but it's your life. You'd better get that gook off your face before it makes you break out. Remember, I told you that it's not really good for your skin."

"O.K., Janet. To tell you the truth, I can't wait to get out of this entire costume. Much as I enjoy its effect on my business life, I must admit, I'm very uncomfortable with the way I feel in it, and I hate living a lie."

Samantha showered and changed into a high-waisted hostess gown in a colorful paisley print. The plunging vee of the neckline met the drawstring of the high waistline, emphasizing the curvaceous lines of her unrestrained breasts. She sprinkled on some cologne, then walked into the kitchen.

Janet looked up and raised her eyebrows incredulously. "My, my, don't we look glamorous. What happened to the efficient business lady who walked through the door thirty minutes ago? Has she deserted us already? Don't tell me the show has been canceled after only one performance."

"Cut it out, Janet. For some reason, I had this overwhelming urge to wear something feminine and attractive. I imagine I must be compensating for a day of ugliness."

"I understand. There's no need to explain. It's just a pity that you're wasting all that glamor on me. If this is how you're going to behave each evening, perhaps I'd better start inviting some dinner guests of the opposite sex. There's no sense in squandering all your beauty. After all, it is after business hours."

"No thanks, Janet. I still don't feel any need

for male companionship; I just wanted to feel feminine again. Now, let's enjoy our dinner and I'll tell you about my new job. Then I'm going to get to bed early. I don't want to be late for work tomorrow morning and I want to be fresh enough to do a good job. I have a feeling Mr. Cory Talbott is going to be a very demanding employer."

Chapter Two

The next morning, Samantha got to work at eight o'clock and found the office deserted except for Billy, the boy from the mail room, who was making his rounds, picking up the tail end of yesterday's mail. He eyed her incredulously.

"What are you doing here so early? The office staff doesn't have to be in until nine."

"It's my first full day on the job and I wanted to be prepared when Mr. Talbott arrives. I certainly want to last longer than those other secretaries I've heard about."

Billy smiled, his candidly appraising glance traveling swiftly down her body. "Don't worry, you're nothing like those other girls. I'm sure Mrs. Harrison and Mr. Talbott will be pleased with you."

Samantha sat back in her seat and raised her eyebrow. "What does Mrs. Harrison have to do with this? I thought I would be working for Cory Talbott. Isn't he the one I have to worry about pleasing?"

Billy laughed and perched himself on the edge of Samantha's desk. "You really are new around here. Let me give you the lowdown. Lavinia Harrison runs this place with an iron hand. Don't believe a word she tells you about it being a one-man operation. Cory Talbott is the brains behind the business. He makes the decisions that affect the finances of some of the wealthiest people in the world, but he just couldn't care less about how this office is run so long as the work gets out. That's where Mrs. Harrison comes in. She's been with him since the year one. She used to be his private secretary, you know. That's why no one else is good enough to do the job. She behaves like a mother hen toward him, very protective, if you know what I mean. So she's the one you'd better watch out for if you want to last around here." He glanced quickly at his watch. "Well, I'd better get going. Yell if you need me."

After he left, Samantha reflected on what Billy had said. As if in response to her thoughts, Mrs. Harrison poked her head through the door.

"My, you're here early. You don't have to be in until nine. It's only eight forty-five, and it appears you've been here for a while."

"I wanted to be here when Mr. Talbott arrived. I thought he might have some work that needed my immediate attention. I didn't want him waiting while I got my things in order."

"A most commendable approach, Miss Lorrimer. Your attitude of total preparedness will be greatly appreciated, I'm sure. I'll check back later to see how things are going."

Samantha spent the next hour going through the file cabinet, familiarizing herself with all facets of the company. She was reaching into the top drawer when Cory Talbott opened the door. She turned from the tall steel cabinet to find him staring at her long slender legs, revealed as she stretched to reach some files. Her face flamed with embarrassment as she quickly moved away from the cabinet and smoothed her skirt. Talbott's eyes whisked from her legs and studied the flustered expression on her face. His gaze seemed to concentrate on her eyes as if they held the key to a puzzle he was trying to unravel.

Then he spoke in his usual subdued manner. "Good morning, Miss Lorrimer. I'm just going to get myself a cup of coffee, then I'd like you to bring in my appointment calendar. I'd like to review my schedule with you."

"Would you like to do that right away, or shall I wait until you've finished your coffee?"

"Now would be fine. Come on in and we can get right to it. Keeping tabs on my appointments is one of the most important functions of your job and I like to begin each day by reviewing them. What do you have listed for today?"

Samantha checked the appointment book in front of her. "Your morning seems to be free. Then Mr. James Carson is scheduled for a luncheon appointment. Shall I make a reservation?"

"Yes, I believe Mrs. Harrison knows which restaurant Mr. Carson is partial to. Why don't you check with her? I don't imagine I have any other appointments scheduled for the remainder of the day. Mr. Carson usually keeps me occupied for the entire day when he flies in from the Coast."

Samantha's eyes opened wide in recognition. "Is this *the* James Carson? I mean, is he the movie actor?"

Cory smiled. "Yes, Miss Lorrimer, this is indeed James Carson the movie actor, idol of millions of starry-eyed women. However, I somehow didn't imagine you would be a part of that thundering herd." He flashed a curious smile at Samantha.

Scarlet flames leapt into Samantha's cheeks. They burned through the gray haze of her make-up, illuminating her face. "I'm not really a fan of his. I guess I'm just surprised that such a famous person should be visiting our office."

Cory leaned back in his chair. "Mr. Carson is not paying a social visit to our office, Miss Lorrimer. He's one of our clients. In fact, we have many well-known people among our clients. I hope you don't intend to blush madly each time one of them schedules an appointment."

Samantha's body stiffened. Cory Talbott was making fun of her, as if he were disappointed that anyone so plainly unattractive could be infatuated with a handsome movie star. "I'm not the type of person to neglect my duties for any reason whatsoever. I can assure you that I will not behave in a manner that will embarass either the firm or its clients."

Samantha slid out of the chair and walked stiffly toward the open door. She could feel Cory's eyes blazing through her back as she closed the door behind her.

Sitting down at her desk, she tried to gather her wits before she checked with Mrs. Harrison and made Cory's luncheon reservations. The colossal nerve of the man, she thought, clenching her fists angrily. Did he expect her to behave like some unfeeling piece of steel machinery? Wouldn't anybody be impressed by the appearance of a famous movie star?

No, she supposed Cory Talbott was too cold and detached to be impressed by anyone. His stature in his own field was so great that movie stars and political figures relied entirely upon him to conduct all their financial affairs. He would probably be unimpressed by royalty. And like as not, he expected the same cold self-assured conduct from her. After all, she had been told often enough that she had really been hired because of her sedate and sober manner.

If she wanted to continue in this job, she had better make her inner emotions conform to the façade she had so carefully constructed. Taking a deep breath, she swiveled her chair in the direction of the telephone and called Mrs. Harrison.

She had just replaced the receiver after calling the restaurant when James Carson came ambling through the door. Samantha steeled herself to act calm, although butterflies were flitting about in her stomach. "Mr. Carson, Mr. Talbott is expecting you. Please have a seat for a moment and I'll tell him you're here."

Cory came out immediately and shook James Carson's hand vigorously. "Jim, it's good to see you again. Come on in and I'll bring you up to date on your financial status. Miss Lorrimer, will you please bring us some coffee? Mr. Carson takes his black. Am I right, Jim?"

"That's right, Cory, I take my coffee like everything else . . . California style."

Cory laughed as he closed the door behind them, and Samantha went to prepare the coffee. It was a simple task since both men took their coffee black. She wondered if Cory Talbott also took everything California style. But then she grimly decided that that was hardly likely. He was far too stiff and formal to be anything but a dyed-in-the-wool New Yorker. There was definitely no breezy California air about him.

She rapped lightly on the door and brought the coffee into Cory's private office. She served James Carson first and couldn't help noticing, when she gave him his coffee, how he stared first at her face and then at her hand. His eyes wandered back to her face, then swept over her entire body as she moved to give Cory his cup.

She felt the heat of an uncontrollable blush explode, and Cory looked up just in time to see the fire spreading through her face. He regarded her with a look of utter contempt as if she had disappointed him by behaving in such a school-girlish manner. Samantha straightened her shoulders and spoke in a carefully controlled voice. "Will there be anything else, Mr. Talbott?"

"Not right now, Miss Lorrimer. Just see that we're not disturbed. I'll buzz you if we need anything."

Silence shrouded the room as Samantha turned and left, closing the door behind her. She sat down at her desk, thoroughly annoyed with herself. What on earth was wrong with her? At last she had the chance she had been waiting for and she was going to lose it because of her ridiculously juvenile behavior. Why was she becoming so flustered? Perhaps Janet was right. Maybe she wasn't meant to be a successful career woman. She was acting as flighty as any of those other girls who had worked for Cory Talbott. What kind of a mess had she created for herself?

A few hours later Cory buzzed Samantha on the intercom. "Miss Lorrimer, have you made my luncheon reservation? We're about ready to leave now."

"Yes, Mr. Talbott, the restaurant is expecting you at twelve-thirty. I'll call and tell them you're on your way."

She was still speaking on the phone when she swiveled in her seat to find Jim Carson's eyes burning into her face. Fortunately, she had achieved some level of composure by this time and was able to squelch the reddening blush before it consumed her body. She smiled sweetly at him in her most decorous manner as she hung up the phone. "Is there anything I can help you with, Mr. Carson?"

"No, not really," he drawled in that western accent for which he was so famous. He sat down on the edge of her desk and examined her face with his steely blue eyes. "I've just been wondering why such an obviously attractive young woman is dressed in ill-fitting, unbecoming clothing and wearing harsh stage makeup in a business office."

Samantha busied herself with some papers on her desk. "I don't know what you're talking about, Mr. Carson."

"Oh, I think you do, Miss Lorrimer. You just don't want to let me in on your little secret. But let me warn you, I'm a very persistent man and I won't rest until I've fished it out of you."

Cory came walking out of the office, shrugging his arms into his expensive mohair jacket. "Come on, Jim. Don't waste your best line on Miss Lorrimer. Save it for those sweet young starlets who don't know any better. It's taken me a long time to find someone as reliable as Miss Lorrimer and I'm not about to have you frighten her off."

Carson smiled knowingly at Samantha. "Don't bother to explain. I think I understand the situation perfectly and I'm intrigued no end. We must make arrangements to get together and discuss this more fully, when we can be alone."

Cory looked at James Carson as if he had lost his mind. "Hey, Jim, I mean it. Stop teasing Miss Lorrimer. She's not your type. Can't you believe that there are some women who are immune to your magical spell?"

"Oh, come on, Cory. You know how much a challenge always appeals to me. I think I'll try to get to know your new girl Friday a little better . . . on her own time, of course."

Cory shook his head and snorted. "Jim, you're incorrigible. Must you make a play for every woman who crosses your path?"

Jim turned and winked at Samantha. "You never know, Cory. Sometimes the most appetizing dishes come served in uninteresting wrappers. You have to cut through the shell to reach the sweet inside. Sort of like a cream puff, if you know what I mean." He followed Cory out the door, leaving Samantha doing a slow burn at her desk.

She was biting her lower lip, trying to regain her composure, when Billy walked into the room. "What happened to you? You're shaking like a leaf."

"James Carson was just in here, and I guess I was unnerved by being so close to a famous person. I can't imagine what got into me; I'm not usually so easily upset."

Billy smiled. "You'd better get used to being around famous people. Mr. Talbott's client list reads like a combination of the social register and the cast of a Hollywood spectacular, with a few well-known sports figures thrown in for good measure. He even manages the investments for several colleges."

"I know. And I think he was a bit annoyed at my reaction to Mr. Carson. I guess he expects me to be some sort of statue, totally unaffected by anything that occurs in this office."

"That's about the size of it. Talbott's the coldest individual I've ever come across. All his decisions are based on facts and figures, and Mrs. Harrison is the same way. I imagine you were chosen for this position because they assumed you were a kindred spirit."

The outer door opened, admitting Mrs. Harrison. She looked coldly at Billy. "Don't you have duties to attend to, Billy?"

With a quick wink at Samantha, Billy was gone.

Mrs. Harrison looked stern. "I should have warned you about Billy. He's the office gossip. I wouldn't listen too much to him if I were you. And how has your morning been?"

"I'm beginning to learn my way around, I think. But I'm afraid I disappointed Mr. Talbott a bit while Mr. Carson was here. It was my first encounter with a celebrity and I was a bit flustered."

Surprisingly, Mrs. Harrison was not annoyed by Samantha's admission. "I can well understand your discomfort, my dear. We should have prepared you for the type of people you'll be seeing in this office. Meeting James Carson up close, unexpectedly, would unnerve any woman, even one as settled as you or I."

Samantha felt her nerves jangle at the comparison between herself and Mrs. Harrison. Why, she thought, Mrs. Harrison *does* believe we're cut from the same piece of cloth—that's why she hired me. "Yes, and I'm sure this will never happen again now that I'm prepared for such encounters."

Mrs. Harrison smiled. "Oh, I'm sure you'll be able to handle the situation admirably. That's why I recommended you for the job. However, I came in to ask if you were busy for lunch. We do get a full hour and I thought you might enjoy dining at a small coffee shop near here which caters to a more refined group than most of the inexpensive dining places in the area."

Samantha saw no way to refuse politely and the two women left together.

Lunch with Mrs. Harrison proved to be a trying experience and Samantha breathed a sigh of relief when once again she entered her own office. Cory Talbott was still out, so she took these few minutes to check her appearance and collect her thoughts. Mrs. Harrison had spent most of the lunch hour discussing Samantha's private life. Samantha could tell that she was trying to discover as much about her background as possible, and kept switching the conversation back to a more general discussion about office procedures, but nonetheless she found the entire experience very unnerving and was determined to avoid Mrs. Harrison as much as possible in the future.

It was late afternoon when Cory and James Carson returned from lunch. Samantha could see that Carson had been drinking, but Cory was as much in control of his senses as ever. He opened the door to his private office and waited for the other man to precede him into the room. Instead, Carson deposited himself on Samantha's desk. "Go ahead, Cory. I'm too looped to think about business now. I want to get to know more about this enticing new secretary of yours."

Cory left the door and walked over to Carson, grasping him firmly by the elbow. Samantha realized that Carson might be the hero of the cinema, but Cory was in complete control of the situation right now. The steely look in his determined eyes caught her by surprise. His voice was cold and imperious. "Let's go, Jim. There's a nice cushiony couch in my office. You can catch a good nap there until you feel better. I meant what I said about leaving Miss Lorrimer alone." He led Carson into his office without a backward glance at Samantha.

In a short while Cory returned to the outer office. "I'm sorry about Mr. Carson's behavior, Miss Lorrimer. I hope he didn't upset you too much. He means no real harm." Pausing for a moment, he narrowed his eyes and peered intently at Samantha's face. "I can't understand why he was bothering you. He likes to tease the young girls in the office, but he's never made a play for Mrs. Harrison and you're certainly more her type than any other."

"Please don't give it another thought," Samantha said. "He was just trying to be nice by making me feel young and attractive. However, I realize my place and I'm not about to be swayed by his smooth manner."

"I'm glad to hear that, Miss Lorrimer. I can't tell you how refreshing it is to have an honest, sensible person in the office again. I never thought I'd find a suitable replacement for Mrs. Harrison until you came along."

Samantha shuddered at the mention of her honesty. Could anything be more deceptive than the charade in which she was engaged? What would Cory think of her if he ever found out her true identity? And how far would James Carson go in his attempt to discover what was really hidden beneath the heavy makeup and ill-fitting clothes?

Cory's calm voice pulled her out of her reverie. "Were there any calls or messages while I was gone?"

Samantha got the pile of phone messages and handed it to Cory. "Mrs. Harrison invited me to join her for lunch and the switchboard took your calls while I was out. I'll check back with them and clear up anything that's confusing."

Cory studied the messages. "Thank you, Miss Lorrimer. Everything's perfectly clear. I have some letters I'd like to dictate, and if things hold true to form, Jim's going to be occupying my office for the rest of the day. So get your steno pad out and I'll grab a chair and start dictating out here."

Samantha spent the remainder of the after-noon taking dictation. When he had finished, he went back into his office, leaving Samantha to type the letters. Glancing quickly at her watch, she saw that it was five o'clock. If she had him sign the letters now she could just get them to the mail room in time for the last mail.

She rapped lightly on Cory's door. When he answered her she walked in, glancing toward the sofa and noting James Carson's prone form still slumbering contentedly.

Cory's eyes followed hers to the sofa, then returned to her face. "What can I do for you, Miss Lorrimer?"

"I thought if you could sign these letters now, we'd get them in the mail tonight."

Samantha handed Cory the letters and her fingers touched his as he reached for them. She quickly pulled her hand away as if she had touched a red-hot flame. Cory's eyes lingered on her hand a moment longer, then drifted slowly to her face, pausing to note the concealed curvaceous scenery along the way. His eyes held a quizzical smile as they froze on hers.

"There's no need to hide your hands, Miss Lorrimer. They're really quite attractive. In fact, they look like the hands of a young girl. Apparently you haven't done much physical labor with them. In any case, you certainly have no cause to be ashamed of them."

Samantha fidgeted nervously under his stare, but was saved from further probing by a drawling voice from the sofa.

"I told you Miss Lorrimer is full of hidden surprises, like soft young hands and long slender legs. I would venture to guess that she might be an ideal candiate for a Pygmalion-style transformation. Would you like to give it a try, Cory?"

Cory looked over at Jim. "Well, I see you've decided to rejoin the world of the living. True to form, the first words out of your mouth concern a member of the opposite sex. I told you before,

Miss Lorrimer is a definite hands off as far as you're concerned."

"All right, Cory, if you feel that strongly about it. But I do believe you're missing the chance of a lifetime. Now, if the mysterious Miss Lorrimer will bring the lecherous Mr. Carson a cup of black coffee, he will be most appreciative."

Samantha was anxious for an excuse to exit the room and she left quickly to get the coffee. She tried to compose herself as she poured the dark, steaming liquid into the cup. Taking a deep breath, she threw back her shoulders, froze her face into a solemnly fixed expression and reentered the office. Jim smiled at her enigmatically as he took the cup from her quaking hands. Samantha turned quickly and walked toward Cory's desk. She stared straight ahead until he finished signing the last of the letters and handed them to her.

"They're all signed and ready to go, Miss Lorrimer. After you give them to Billy, you may leave. I don't believe I have any other work which requires your immediate attention."

Samantha nodded eagerly; she was glad to get away from Jim Carson's knowing eyes, and she had a night-school class to get to anyway.

Night school was taxing after a full day's work and Samantha was really exhausted when she let herself into the apartment.

Janet called out from the kitchen, "Is that you, Sam? Come on into the kitchen." She looked up as Samantha walked into the room. "Gad, you look awful. Wash that makeup off your face. I think you're starting to break out from it. Why on earth didn't you wash it off before you went to class?"

Samantha went into the bathroom and began creaming the makeup off her face. "I was late getting to class and I didn't have time to remove it. But you're right. My skin is beginning to bother me." She put on a long cotton robe and soft white scuffs before sitting down at the table opposite Janet and reaching for a waiting sandwich. "Thanks, Janet. I'm so tired, I doubt that I would have had the energy to make anything for myself."

"Well, I'm happy for your company, Sam. I've been studying for this part in a new play that's opening in the fall. James Carson is starring in it. It's his first time on Broadway and I'm sure the show is going to be a smash. I'd give anything to get the part. It would be just the break I've been waiting for."

Samantha spoke without thinking. "So that's why he's in town."

"That's why who's in town? What are you talking about, Samantha?"

"James Carson. He was in our office today. Cory manages his money."

"James Carson was in your office? You actually spoke to him? Samantha, answer me!"

"Yes, I spoke to him . . . sort of."

Janet's eyes were alight. "Sam, you know James Carson? Please, can you put in a good word for me? I know I can get the part if he just notices me. I've been studying it all week, but you know what happens at these auditons. There are so many other beautiful girls that it's hard to be noticed. If James Carson was watching out for me, I'm sure I'd stand a better chance of getting the part. You've got to help me, Sam. Please."

"I don't know what I can do, Janet. I hardly know the man. He just thinks of me as Cory Talbott's secretary, although I think he may suspect something about the makeup. I can't take the chance that he might discover who I really am."

Janet refused to be put off. "Look, can't I meet you for lunch or something? I mean, isn't there some way you can introduce me to him or put in a good word for me? I really want that part."

Samantha thought for a moment. "Gee, Janet, I don't know what I can do. I don't think Mr. Carson is coming to the office tomorrow and if I try to speak to Mr. Talbott about it, I'll be out on my ear without helping you at all. But, I promise, I'll try to think of something and I'll help you out if I can. You're my best friend, Janet. You know I'd do anything to help you."

Chapter Three

Samantha reached the office early the next morning. The mail had not yet arrived and there was very little for her to do. Rather than sit idly, waiting for the telephone to ring, she took out her textbook and began reading her next assignment. She was deeply engrossed in note taking and trying to comprehend some highly technical material when the door to the outer office opened. She looked up, expecting to see Billy or Mrs. Harrison; instead, she was greeted by Cory Talbott's resonant voice.

"Good morning, Miss Lorrimer. You're in rather early, aren't you?" he said as he walked toward her desk.

"I like to get in early. It gives me a chance to get organized. I imagine you're the one who's here unusually early today. Mrs. Harrison said that you generally don't arrive before nine forty-five."

"That's quite true," Cory said, fingering Samantha's textbook. "But if you recall, when I hired you I indicated that we had no set hours and worked as the occasion demanded." He held up the book. "Why are you reading this book on security analysis? It's highly technical. Are you able to understand it?"

"Not all of it. I find some of it too difficult when I first read it, but I'm taking a course and I'll understand it better after the instructor explains it to the class."

Cory tilted his head and narrowed his eyes. "This is a bit deep for a secretary, isn't it? How long have you been taking courses and just what are your career intentions?"

Samantha thought carefully about her answer. This was her opportunity to tell Cory about her ambition to make it in the financial industry. If she chose her words carefully, she could make him realize that she wanted more out of life than a secretarial career. Thanks to her elaborate disguise, she was at last being taken seriously, and she was not about to waste this marvelous chance to declare her intentions. "I've been taking classes since I first came to New York, two years ago. Ultimately, I'd like to do financial planning and analysis. I hope to be able to move away from a secretarial position after I've completed sufficient courses."

"Well, Miss Lorrimer, I become more impressed with your talents with each passing moment. I studied security analysis under the author of this book when I was at Harvard Business School and I'm quite familiar with his methods. I'd be very happy to explain anything you have difficulty understanding."

He headed toward his private office, then turned and flashed a compelling smile at Samantha. "However, I must tell you, I'm not at all pleased at the thought of losing a competent secretary, since it's taken me so long to find one. Perhaps we could promote you to my assistant and keep you on in that capacity. We'll have to sit down and discuss it someday when you're further along in your studies. In any case, today is going to be a very busy one. Silver prices are fluctuating on the London Exchange and I have a number of clients who would be interested in buying if the price drops low enough. Call our man in London so I can discuss the situation with him."

Samantha placed the call, buzzing through to Cory when his party was on the line. She had just replaced the receiver when the telephone rang. She answered it and recognized Janet's voice at the other end.

"Sam, have you had a chance to speak to James Carson?"

"Janet, are you mad? It's only eight-thirty in the morning. I doubt if James Carson is even out of bed. Besides, involving clients in one's personal affairs is strictly prohibited."

"All right, but if you can speak to him or even to Mr. Talbott, I'd appreciate it. This is really important. Well, I'm going to leave now. I want to get there early so I have a chance to size up the opposition."

"Good luck, Janet, and if I can do anything I will."

The intercom buzzed almost immediately and she answered Cory's call.

His voice came through the speaker with the deeply commanding resonance she had already come to associate with him. "Please come into my office, Miss Lorrimer. I have some things that require your immediate attention."

Samantha rose from her chair and entered the private office. Cory's normally tidy desk was a blizzard of disorderly papers. He was speaking on the phone and plotting some numbers on a graph. He motioned for Samantha to approach the desk, covered the telephone receiver and handed her a sheet of paper.

"Call the people on this list immediately. Tell them the current price of silver and see if they want me to buy them the amount of ounces I've indicated next to each name. Then get back to me as soon as possible." Motioning her away, he returned to his conversation.

They spent the entire day at their desks. Samantha was kept busy performing the tasks Cory requested of her and he was constantly on the phone, checking prices and confirming sales. Samantha called out for sandwiches at twelve o'clock and they ate lunch at their desks, working straight through until eight in the evening. She realized she had missed her night-school class and brushed it off, deciding that she had probably learned more about the world of high finance today than she would ever learn in any classroom.

She heaved a sigh and straightened the huge stack of papers on her desk, smiling to herself as she thought how deceptively quiet the day had been at the start. When her desk was as orderly as possible under the circumstances, she rapped lightly on the door to Cory's private office. He was leaning back in his chair, his arms clasped comfortably behind his head. His expensive silk tie hung loosely about his unbuttoned collar, revealing the dark, softly curling hair on his muscular chest. A contented smile played over his relaxed lips, making him seem totally different from the impersonal, dynamic machine Samantha had been working with all day.

He straightened up and let his arms drop to the desk. "Well, Miss Lorrimer, we've had a most successful day. Talbott Associates has made quite a bit of money for its clients, which, of course, is what they pay us to do, and I appreciate all the help you've given me. I realize you've worked straight through lunch and now it's eight o'clock and you haven't had any dinner. Did you have anything scheduled for this evening?"

Samantha smiled. "Well, I did have a class at six-thirty, but I'm sure I learned more about financial transactions today in the office than I would have learned in a month of classes. I just hope the instructor will review the chapter on balance-sheet analysis. I still find it a bit confusing. It seems to me you'd have to be an accountant to really understand what the figures mean."

Cory smiled. "Why, Miss Lorrimer, do you mean there's something you don't know how to do? You handled everything with such perfect precision today that I thought nothing was beyond your capabilities." His gray eyes twinkled with amusement. "Since you've missed both your dinner and your class on my account, I feel obligated to make proper amends for both losses. So, I'll take you to dinner and while we're eating I'll explain the intricacies of the balance sheet to you."

Samantha blushed. She was anxious to get home and wash off her makeup, which was beginning to make her face itch badly. "There's no need to take me to dinner, Mr. Talbott. I was merely doing my job and, as I said, I probably learned more today than I ever would have learned in my night-school class."

Cory smiled. "I insist you let me take you to dinner and impress you with my knowledge of the world of high finance. Now go freshen up while I make reservations, and don't let me hear any further protests. When you've worked for me a bit longer, you'll know I always insist upon having my own way."

Samantha smiled and walked out the door. The only freshening up she wanted to do was to wash the thick layer of makeup off her face and get out of her stiff, unsightly clothing. She hadn't the slightest desire to be seen in public in this horrible costume, but there was no way she could discard it as long as she was in the company of Cory Talbott. The bridge of her nose was beginning to ache from the weight of the heavy horn-rimmed glasses, but she couldn't remove them either. She was completely trapped by her own falsehoods. Her only hope was that Cory would conclude the dinner quickly. She was sure he had no desire to remain in her company any longer than was necessary and was just inviting her to dinner out of politeness. When she returned to the office, Cory was sitting on the edge of her desk, waiting for her.

"Everything's all set. I was able to get reservations at a wonderful French restaurant near Broadway. It's a favorite actors' hangout, and we'll be able to enjoy dinner without being rushed."

When they reached the basement garage, he directed Samantha toward a maroon Jaguar sports model. He opened the door and waited while she settled herself in the passenger seat, then shut the door and walked to the driver's side. "I guess it's silly to own a car like this in New York, where you're lucky if the traffic moves at five miles an hour, but when I was in college upstate I used to enjoy the races at Watkins Glen and I love driving a powerful automobile."

He drove slowly through the deserted financial district. "It's funny how this place dies each evening. People make their money here during the day and spend it on Broadway after dark."

Samantha couldn't help but admit the truth of his statement as they neared the theater district.

Garish lights illuminated the evening darkness, making their own private form of artificial sunshine. Cory stopped the car in front of a navy blue canvas canopy. A doorman hastened to open Samantha's door and Cory handed his car keys to the parking attendant. They both greeted Cory by name, making it obvious to Samantha that he was a frequent patron of this restaurant.

The doorman held the door and Cory ushered Samantha in, putting his hand on her shoulder to guide her. An involuntary quiver ran up Samantha's spine at his possessive touch and Cory immediately withdrew his hand.

"Sorry, Miss Lorrimer. I didn't mean to upset you. I keep forgetting how jumpy you are around men. I guess I've just become used to you after being so close all day."

Samantha nodded her head ineffectively. Her little deception was becoming more involved with each passing minute. She looked up as the maître d' approached them. He eyed Samantha curiously, then greeted Cory with a warm smile.

"So good to see you again, Mr. Talbott. I have your table all ready for you."

"Thank you, Henri. This is Miss Lorrimer, my secretary."

Samantha smiled, nodding her head in Henri's direction. She could see the glimmer of understanding flash across his face.

Convinced that Samantha was no more than a paid employee, Henri addressed himself to Cory. "I was surprised to see you here without Miss Gerard, but now I understand."

Cory smiled. "Miss Gerard has taken herself to

a spa in California, so I'm on my own for a few weeks. I imagine I'll have to get used to lonely bachelor dinners, and you know how much I detest eating alone, so I'm grateful that Miss Lorrimer has honored me with her presence tonight."

Samantha followed Henri over the plush red carpet to a table in a secluded area at the side of the room. She watched as he removed the reserved sign and held the chair out for her.

Cory shrugged away the menu Henri offered. "Just bring us two glasses of Chablis; we need some time to unwind. Then, if Miss Lorrimer will trust my judgment, I'll order for both of us."

Samantha nodded gratefully. The less she had to do, the better. Her skin was beginning to itch unbearably and the pressure of her eyeglasses on the bridge of her nose was making her wince in pain. She prayed that the evening would end quickly. However, it was apparent that Cory was a gracious host, no matter who he was entertaining, and he had obviously decided to perform an act of charity by bringing a bit of elegance into her dismal life.

Gratefully, she curved her hand around the chilled wineglass when it arrived at the table. She couldn't imagine how Cory could possibly have known that a mild white Chablis was her favorite alcoholic beverage. She had closed her eyes and was trying to visualize the hot bubble bath she was going to pour herself into as soon as she got home when she was startled out of her reverie by an all-too familiar voice.

"Cory Talbott, fancy meeting you here, and

with my favorite secretary, too. I hear I made a killing in the silver market today. Is that what you two are celebrating?"

"Not at all, Jim. Miss Lorrimer and I have been working hard all day on those silver purchases, foregoing a decent lunch. In addition, Miss Lorrimer missed her night-school class, and since I decided we both deserved a relaxing dinner, we came here. Now, if you'll go to your own table, we'll finish our wine and order our dinner."

"Not at all! I won't hear of it! Since you two have been working desperately all day just to increase the amount of gold in my coffers, the very least I can do in return is treat you to dinner. My lovely companion has just gone to powder her nose and will be joining us shortly. Then we can all enjoy a relaxing dinner." He signaled for Henri to add two more place settings to the table and sat down next to Samantha.

Just when Samantha thought that nothing more could happen to increase her discomfort, Cory and Jim stood up to greet Jim's date. Samantha gasped audibly as Jim spoke.

"Cory, I'd like you to meet Janet Rogers, my latest discovery." He smiled down at Samantha's stricken face. "I believe you already know Miss Rogers."

Samantha looked up at Janet, who was obviously as startled as she was. However, her professional training was readily apparent as Janet's face quickly became expressionless and she nodded confidently at Samantha, indicating that she had the situation under control. Cory looked at Janet with undisguised amazement. Her long ebony hair swirled about her face and shoulders, providing the perfect foil for the stark simplicity of her spaghetti-strapped, white silk sheath. Then, as if he didn't trust his ears, he lowered his eyes to compare this vision of beauty with the dour simplicity of his secretary. Samantha, catching his incredulous gaze, cast her eyes down in embarrassed silence.

Janet slithered into her chair, smiling sweetly while the two men reseated themselves. Then, speaking in her most professionally modulated tones, she said, "Just imagine my surprise this morning when, arriving early at the audition, I struck up a casual conversation with Jim, only to find that he was acquainted with my roommate."

Cory was bewildered. "You and Miss Lorrimer room together?"

Jim leaned back in his seat, grinning. "Yes, you can imagine how amazed I was when Janet mentioned that we had a mutual acquaintance. Although I must admit, I wasn't half as surprised as you appear to be, Cory. I believe this is the only time I've ever seen the totally self-controlled Cory Talbott at a loss for words. What's wrong, Cory? Don't the facts and figures add up?"

Cory was visibly annoyed at being caught off guard. "I think it's perfectly natural for me to be surprised when a client's date turns out to be my secretary's roommate. You must admit the coincidence is a bit startling."

Jim smiled at Cory with the look of a man who knew a secret he wasn't about to share. "I don't know why the situation should surprise you. There's nothing that unusual about two beautiful unmarried ladies sharing an apartment."

Cory had now fully recovered from his initial shock and was not about to put up with any more of Jim's pointed barbs. "I'm perfectly aware of my dinner guest's many charms, having spent the last twelve hours in her company, and by just looking at Miss Rogers I can see that she is equally charming, so I'm delighted to find that they know each other so well. Now, if you don't mind, I would like to order dinner. I promised Miss Lorrimer a relaxing evening and so far it's been anything but." Raising his hand, he signaled to the waiter, who immediately approached the table.

Cory lowered his eyes and directed them toward Jim as the waiter lifted his order pad. "I'm ordering for Miss Lorrimer and myself. Would you like me to order for you and Miss Rogers?"

Jim glanced at Janet to get her approval. She nodded her head and flashed her blinding smile, speaking sweetly to Cory. "I'm sure that would be fine, Mr. Talbott, and please call me Janet; Miss Rogers sounds so formal."

The meal Cory had chosen started with a rich onion soup, swimming in croutons and baked Parmesan cheese. The main dish was crisp duckling in orange sauce, accompanied by steamed, buttered vegetables. Samantha hadn't realized how hungry she was and enjoyed her food immensely. She looked up to see Cory watching her with amusement when he asked if she would like something from the pastry cart. She chose a flaky cream puff, covered with chocolate sauce, and sat back to enjoy it with a steaming cup of rich black coffee.

Cory was still studying her when she finished her dessert. "Miss Lorrimer, you make me feel that my money has been well spent. I can't tell you how much I detest ordering a good dinner for someone, only to have her pick at it and return the better part of her meal to the kitchen untouched."

Jim raised an eyebrow and looked at Samantha. "I agree with you, Cory; Samantha is a gem among women and you'd be a fool to let her go. However, the dinner is my treat, so we must consider that it's been my money that was well spent."

Cory nodded appreciatively in Jim's direction. "Thank you, Jim. You've been a generous, gracious host. Now, since Miss Lorrimer and I have a full day of work before us tomorrow, we'd best take our leave of you two charming night owls. Actors may sleep till noon, but the stock market opens at ten, and we must be wide awake well before then."

He held Samantha's chair while she rose, then flashed a devastating smile in Janet's direction. "It was nice meeting you, Janet. I'm sure we'll be seeing more of each other." He placed his hand on Samantha's waist as she mumbled her good-byes and guided her firmly toward the door.

His car was waiting when they approached the canopy. Cory let the doorman seat Samantha, then got behind the wheel and turned to her. "Do you feel like going for a short drive to unwind, or are you anxious to get home?"

Samantha nibbled nervously at her lower lip. If she didn't get into a warm tub soon, she was going to fall completely apart. It would take just the slightest bit of encouragement from Cory Talbott to make her confess the entire unsavory scheme and throw herself on his nonexistent mercy. She sincerely doubted that the Wizard of Wall Street would be amused at finding himself her dupe. She meekly lowered her head, not daring to look in his direction. "I'm really tired. This entire day has been quite an experience for me. I can't wait to get home and relax in a warm tub."

"Your wish is my command. There's absolutely no need to be apologetic about it. However, I do owe you a lesson on balance sheets, but we'll take a raincheck on it until you're more wide awake. Now, just give me directions to your apartment and my magic chariot will have you home in a flash."

Samantha directed Cory to her apartment house and he double-parked the car in front of her building. She thanked him for the dinner and prepared to leave the car, but he motioned her to remain seated and came around to open the door for her. Then he began to follow her into the building.

"Please, don't bother to walk me to the door. I'll be all right. I'm used to coming home from school by myself at night. You'll probably get a parking ticket if you leave the car where it is."

"Nonsense; I won't have you walking into the house by yourself. I'll see you to your door. Let me worry about the parking tickets."

He reached for her hand and began turning it over in his. Lightly, his fingers traced the inner curve of her palm. Little shivers ran races on Samantha's spine, and her heart began to thud wildly. Quickly, she pulled her hand away.

Cory's eyes flashed over her face thoughtfully. "You can come in late tomorrow morning. You've had a full day today and deserve a few extra hours of sleep tomorrow." He waved good-bye and walked quickly down the stairs.

Samantha bolted the door behind him and removed her heavy glasses. She walked into the bedroom and began stripping off her clothes. When she was clad only in her half slip and bra, she creamed the makeup off her face and glanced uneasily at her blotchy complexion, realizing that her delicate skin was reacting poorly to the daily dose of greasy stage makeup. She turned the taps of the tub on full blast, added some perfumed bubble bath to the warm water and sank contentedly into its steamy depths.

Closing her eyes, she enjoyed the scented warmth of the relaxing water and reflected on the activities of the day. Almost immediately she began thinking about Cory Talbott. When he took her hand . . . Just thinking about it made her blush. Cory Talbott was everything she had ever wanted in an employer and, she smiled wryly, he was everything she had ever wanted in a man. Scooping up a handful of bubbles, she ran them lightly over her arm and tried to imagine Cory's fingers drifting from her palm to her shoulder to her body—she sat up abruptly. What on earth was wrong with her? She had finally found an employer who treated her with respect and she was mooning over him like a lovesick schoolgirl. This turn of events would be funny if it wasn't so downright dangerous. Cory Talbott could never become romantically interested in her, so she had just better get her own wild emotions back in touch with reality.

Rising from the cooling tub, she patted herself dry with a fluffy turkish towel, put on a short terry robe and went into the living room. She was much too tired to do any studying, but she was too tense from the excitement of the day to fall asleep immediately, so she decided to lie down on the couch and watch a late-night movie. She was nearly dozing when she heard Janet's key in the door. She was too tired to move and lay where she was, waiting for Janet to enter the apartment.

Janet came gliding into the living room, but she wasn't alone—Jim Carson was with her. He took one look at Samantha stretched out on the sofa and gave a long, low whistle. "You really *are* Cinderella!"

Samantha sat up quickly, tucking her legs under her to hide them. However, her embarrassment left him completely unperturbed. He sank into the downy cushions of an arm chair and stretched his long legs in front of him. Janet sat on the arm of the chair as he placed his hand on her waist. She looked at Samantha uneasily.

"Please don't be upset, Sam. I told Jim all

about your predicament. He already suspected something and I merely clarified the situation for him." She looked at Samantha's disconsolate face. "Sam, stop being so unhappy. Jim has promised to keep our secret. You have nothing to worry about. I never would have told him if I felt we couldn't trust him. You know I value your friendship more than that."

Jim's expression turned serious. "What she says is true, Samantha. Don't be misled by the things you've heard about me, or even by the way you've seen me behave in Cory's presence. I'm really just a small-town boy who got a lucky break in the movie industry. But I never forget my origins and the most fun I know is to go back home to the Ozark Mountains, stay in my three-room cabin and fish and hunt. Incidentally, I wasn't as looped as you thought I was the other day. I'm just a very good actor and I enjoy putting Cory Talbott on. He's one of the nicest people I know, but he's so straightlaced he drives me crazy. That's why I'm so delighted to hear about your little scheme. Maybe Cory will loosen up when he finds out how he's been tricked."

Samantha gasped. "No! He mustn't find out. He'd never forgive me. I feel awful about what I've done. Promise me that you'll never tell him." Her voice hovered between anger and tears.

Jim's face softened. "Take it easy, Samantha. I'm not about to do anything to upset you." His eyes moved up to rest on Janet as he tightened his hold on her waist. "And I'm certainly not about to do anything to make Janet angry with me. I won't say anything to Cory if you don't want me to, but you're not going to be able to keep wearing that makeup much longer; look at how your face is breaking out."

Samantha was close to tears. "I don't know what to do. I really like my job. Working with Cory is wonderful. He treats me like a person with a mind, not just an empty-headed piece of flesh. But I know I can't keep wearing this makeup and I don't know what will happen when he finds out the truth."

Janet sighed. "I think you're making more of this than it is, Samantha. Jim is sure that Cory thinks enough of you now not to dismiss you when he finds out what you've done. Besides, you had a very good reason for doing it; it wasn't just an idle prank. I'm sure Cory will be able to understand that."

Samantha shook her head unhappily. "I don't think so. He sets great value on honesty. I don't think he'll understand my deception at all, no matter what my reason is. I just don't know what I'm going to do."

"Well, one thing's for sure, you can't go on wearing that makeup. But your skin looks so bad right now that I don't think it needs any makeup to make it look worse. Just place a little over the nose hump to disguise it and leave the rest of your face alone. The glasses and the blotchy skin will be unattractive enough by themselves."

Jim rose from his chair, giving Janet's shoulder a little squeeze. "Janet's right, Samantha.

The worst thing that can happen is you'll lose your job, and if that happens I'll use my contacts to find you another one." He put out his hand to Janet. "Now I'll let you girls get to sleep. I'll see you for lunch tomorrow, Janet."

Samantha had set the alarm for six the next morning, so she arrived at the office by eight o'clock and began going through the huge pile of papers that covered Cory's desk. She wanted to be sure that everything was orderly when Cory arrived so he could get to work immediately. She was separating the orders into those that had been executed and those that were still pending when Mrs. Harrison came into the office.

She handed Samantha some paperwork to be done later in the day, and turned to leave. Then she pivoted hesitantly, as if unsure about expressing herself. "I don't suppose it's any of my business, Miss Lorrimer, but I couldn't help noticing that you're not wearing your heavy makeup today."

Samantha's heart froze as she saw her doom spelled out before her eyes, but Mrs. Harrison continued speaking in an unusually compassionate voice.

"I can see now why you felt it might be advisable to cover your skin with a heavy coat of makeup but I hope you realize that it isn't necessary in your present position. Mr. Talbott didn't hire you for your cover-girl complexion. As I told you earlier, he doesn't believe in mixing business with pleasure and is never affected by the attractiveness of his female staff. So there is no need for you to hide your poor complexion under layers of heavy makeup. I hope I haven't offended you. I detest mentioning personal things in the office, but I did want you to know that we're so pleased with your work that your appearance is unimportant." Then she left before Samantha could say anything.

Samantha's mouth hung open in amazement. Suddenly, the door opened and Cory Talbott strode into the room. His face was freshly shaven and a faint spicy odor of cologne drifted toward Samantha as he neared her desk. The dark hair at the nape of his neck grazed the soft white silk collar of his shirt and blended into the deep blue of his mohair suit.

"Good morning, Miss Lorrimer." His eyes drifted over her face and she knew he was noticing the difference in her appearance, but he was too polite to mention it to her, and without another word, he disappeared quietly into his private office.

The day passed quickly and Samantha was completely unaware of the time when Cory came into her office.

"It's five o'clock, Miss Lorrimer. Do you have class this evening?"

"No, I can stay late tonight if you need me."

"That won't be necessary. We seem to be pretty well caught up. I was just thinking that this would be a good time for me to fulfill my promises to help you with your schoolwork and take you to dinner. If it's all right with you, I'd be happy to honor my commitment tonight."

Samantha thought this was as good a time as

any. Cory had said that Denise was in California and he hated dining alone. She imagined he wanted to get his obligation to her settled before Denise returned. So she nodded her head in agreement.

Cory broke into a pleased smile. "Good. I'll make arrangements for dinner and we can leave shortly." He disappeared into his office.

Chapter Four

"Well," Cory said, smiling as he returned, "everything has been taken care of and we're free to leave. Remember to bring your book with you."

Samantha pulled the textbook out of the bulging leather satchel that served her as both brief-case and purse and held it up for Cory to see.

She sat quietly while he drove uptown, away from lower Manhattan and Wall Street. She wondered where they were going to eat and assumed it would probably be a fabulously expensive uptown restaurant. She cringed at the thought of appearing once again before all those beautiful people in her unattractive clothing. However, she realized Cory was not going to change his dining habits on her account. He kept riving uptown until they had reached Central Park, then he turned the car into the underground garage of one of the oldest cooperative apartment buildings in New York City. Samantha knew that many famous people had apartments in this building and securing one necessitated the approval of the other owner-tenants.

Although the building was old, the immense wealth of its occupant-owners had enabled them to maintain it as if it had just been built. The individual apartments were constantly being redecorated to suit the needs of the residents and the exterior as well as the interior common areas were kept in good repair by using the plentiful money in the building's mutual fund.

Samantha wondered what they were doing here. She doubted that it could possibly house any commercial restaurant facilities.

Cory pulled the car into a numbered spot and turned to address her as he came around to open her door. "I've taken the liberty of having my cook prepare a dinner for us. I thought it would be more relaxing and I would have more time to spend teaching you about balance sheets. I can't conceive of any restaurant being quiet enough and having enough light for us to accomplish that."

Samantha watched while he guided her to the elevator and nodded to the operator. The man pushed a button marked penthouse and they began the long, direct ascent to the uppermost floor of the building.

They entered a small elegant private lobby

with only one door leading from it. The walls were covered in gold silk and the floor was tiled with alternating squares of black and white marble. It was tastefully furnished with small groupings of antique French furniture painted soft ivory or finished in muted gold leaf. Cory placed his hand on Samantha's waist, barely touching her, yet resting it just lightly enough to steer her to the ivory-and-gold-paneled door leading off the entry. In a moment they had entered the living room, which was dominated by a huge carved-walnut fireplace, filled with greenery now in the intense heat and humidity of the stifling New York summer.

"I'll let my housekeeper know we've arrived. Make yourself comfortable; I'll only be a minute."

Samantha walked to the long row of French doors that lined the opposite wall. They were tightly closed to retain the air-conditioned coolness and shut out the oppressive late August heat of the sweltering city. However, their sparkling leaded-glass panes afforded a panoramic view of the trees and flowers that filled the outside terrace. Samantha was astounded; she couldn't believe that a garden like this existed in the dirt and soot of the city. Cory returned to see her staring at the garden in open amazement.

He moved to stand quietly beside her. "It's beautiful, isn't it? I especially enjoy sitting outside in the spring when the humidity isn't so bad. If it cools off after dinner, perhaps we can have our coffee out there. The terrace has a wonderful view of the park and the museums are just across the street. Would you like to wash before dinner?" He motioned toward the small hallway. "The powder room is through there."

Samantha closed the door of the powder room and examined her reflection in the mirror. The unsightly blotches on her face were still evident, although her skin was no longer tender to the touch. She caught up the few wisps of stray hair that had escaped from her bun and resecured them at the back of her head. She considered removing her navy blue linen suit jacket, but decided against it, thinking that it helped conceal any sensuous curves the thin fabric of her severe white cotton blouse might inadvertently reveal.

Convinced that she still maintained the image of a staid and proper secretary, she returned to the living room. Cory was standing behind a full bar that had previously been hidden beneath the thick walnut paneling. He looked up from the drink he was mixing and addressed Samantha.

"Would you care for a martini?"

Samantha shook her head. "No thanks. I need a clear head if I'm to understand anything about balance sheets. I'm finding them difficult enough already."

Cory laughed. "Don't worry, I promise you'll be as knowledgeable as an accountant before the evening is over. Would you like some sherry? It will whet your appetite for dinner and allow you to keep your wits about you at the same time."

Samantha nodded her head. "Sherry would be fine, thank you."

Cory gave Samantha her sherry and sat down opposite her. "Dinner will be ready shortly. Why don't you tell me a little about yourself? Despite our intimate working arrangement, I find I know very little about your background."

"There's not much to tell," said Samantha, slipping into the truth without thinking. "My father has a small dairy farm in upstate New York. Ever since I can remember I've kept his books for him and prepared his work for the accountant. I got very interested in finances and wanted to go on in the field. But that was hardly possible in the small community where I lived. So, I decided I would give Wall Street a try."

Cory frowned. "I thought Mrs. Harrison said you had been caring for an invalid relative." He slowly twirled his glass and looked directly at Samantha, a confused scowl mounting in the depths of his cool gray eyes. Then, as if he had suddenly reached a decision, he shrugged his shoulders and sipped his drink. "It's unimportant, in any case; the important thing is that you're so marvelously suited for the position and I'm very fortunate to have found you." He smiled pleasantly at Samantha, the scowl in his eyes replaced by a friendly twinkle.

Terrance, Cory's butler and valet, announced that dinner was served and Samantha felt she had been given a reprieve.

Cory motioned the butler away, led Samantha to the dining room, then held out her chair before taking his own seat at the small circular table near the terrace window. Samantha was surprised to find that the large room was furnished with a number of small round tables. She had been expecting a huge dining table where one could barely see from one end to the other.

Cory apparently noticed her suprise and his low voice brought her out of her reverie. "Do you like it? When I was having the apartment decorated, I decided I didn't want to have one of those formal dining tables where you can't see or hear the guests at the opposite end. It would be especially depressing on an occasion like this, when there are only two people dining, so I was delighted when the decorator suggested this arrangement."

"It's lovely," Samantha said while her eyes continued to study the room. A Carrara marble fireplace was set into one richly paneled rosewood wall. Several antique bronze sconces had been electrified, diffusing a soft amber light throughout the room. Their dining table was covered by a floor-length striped silk cloth with a small square of soft white batiste placed over it; the crisply folded table napkins were made of the same white batiste. Two small silver candlesticks graced the table, their long flickering tapers casting ominous shadows over Cory's dark face. Samantha gave an uncontrollable shiver as she studied his aquiline features.

Cory eyed her with surprise. "You're not cold, are you? It's over ninety degrees outside, but I suppose the air-conditioning may be making this place a bit too chilly for you."

Samantha shook her head, not wanting him to know the strange effect his presence was having on her senses. "No, the air-conditioning is fine. It was nothing."

The first course was an icy lobster bisque and it was so delicious that Samantha finished it completely, savoring every drop.

The main course was thin slices of baby veal sautéed in a mild lemon sauce. Cory served a white Riesling wine, and Samantha restricted her intake, claiming once again that she needed a clear head for her studies.

Cory suggested they take their coffee in the living room so they could have it available while they were working. It was still far too humid to venture out onto the terrace. Samantha preceded him into the living room, where Terrance had placed a large silver tray with coffee and small French pastries. Cory told the butler that as soon as he and his wife had finished their chores in the kitchen, they could return to their apartment on the lower floor. Then he turned to Samantha.

"Now let's have a look at the work you're finding so difficult."

Samantha was seated on the sofa. Moving the coffee tray aside, Cory came to sit beside her as she placed the open book on the table. She tensed and moved away as the spicy scent of his cologne drifted toward her, making hidden butterflies flutter beneath her racing heart.

Cory seemed oblivious to Samantha's discomfort and began to explain the information to her. She forced herself to pay attention and listen to what he was saying, but his presence was an almost overpowering distraction. She bent over the book, making a concentrated effort to understand what he was telling her. When he saw her leaning intently over the book he sat closer to her, his long, tapering finger pointing out specific information on the textbook pages. She was heady with the nearness of him when suddenly the room was plunged into darkness. Samantha gasped.

Cory gripped her by the shoulders. "Don't be frightened. We've probably tripped the circuit breaker. I'll go check it out. You stay put; I'll be right back."

Samantha leaned back on the sofa, breathing a deep sigh of relief. She was totally confused by her body's involuntary sensual response to Cory's presence. All her life she had been evading the romantic overtures of demanding men. Now, at last, she had met someone who was interested only in her mind, finding her totally unattractive physically, and her own desires were threatening to run away with her. Cory thought she was homely, and, besides, he was engaged to Denise Gerard. Why must the first man she found emotionally and physically appealing be so utterly unattainable? Ruefully, she remembered an old maxim her mother was fond of quoting about people always wanting what they could not have.

The sound of footsteps cut through the darkness and she turned toward Cory's exasperated voice. "Well, it's not a circuit breaker. I'm afraid we're experiencing another one of New York's famous blackouts. The old electrical system in this city is simply not equipped to carry the load of all these modern appliances. Every time the temperature rises and people turn on their air-conditioners, we overload the generators and black out the city."

The air in the apartment was fast becoming hot and stuffy. Samantha removed her jacket and opened the neck of her blouse, seeking some relief from the oppressive heat. Leaning forward in the darkness, she picked up her book, closed it, and placed it in her handbag. "I don't imagine we'll be doing any more studying tonight, so I might as well be going. It doesn't seem as if I'm ever going to learn about balance sheets."

Cory spoke softly in the darkness. "I'm afraid you're stuck here for the time being. The elevators aren't running and it's a twenty-floor hike to ground level. The best thing we can do is make ourselves comfortable and wait it out." He took off his jacket and loosened his tie, ripping it away from his collar. Then he reached for Samantha's hand. "Come on. We'll roast in here without the air-conditioning. I promised you a tour of the terrace and this seems to be as good a time as any for it. Maybe if we're lucky we'll catch a cool breeze." He led Samantha toward the French doors and opened them.

The air on the terrace was as hot and humid as the steam rising from a Yellowstone geyser. It enveloped anyone who dared venture into its torrid depths, but the lush greenery flourished in the humid heat as if it were in some tender hothouse nursery.

Samantha released herself from Cory's grip, walked to the edge of the terrace and looked

down at the deserted street below. Everything
was in darkness except for a few slowly moving
vehicles on the mostly abandoned roads. Driving was dangerous because the traffic lights,
controlled by electricity, were not working. Samantha tensed as she felt Cory move next to her.
Her eyes remained glued to the quiet streets.
"Everything looks so eerie, doesn't it? It gives
me the shivers just to be out here. I feel so
alone." She drew her arms across her chest as if
to protect herself from some unknown danger
lurking in the darkness.

Cory's arm went around her shoulder in an
almost paternal manner. "There's no need to be
afraid. You're not alone; I'm here, and I out-
grew my fear of the darkness years ago." He
gave Samantha's shoulder a gentle squeeze.
"Let's make ourselves comfortable and we
can relax and get to know more about each
other."

Samantha followed him and sat on a lounge
next to the one he had chosen for himself. The
last thing she wanted was for him to get to know
her better. She only hoped he wouldn't ask any
more pointed questions about her private life
until tomorrow morning. Her deception was becoming so distasteful to her that she longed to
share the truth with him, but she just couldn't
chance his reaction now, when their relationship seemed so comfortable. He so believed in
honesty that he would never understand what
she had done. She was finding it difficult enough
to live with his indifference; how would she
ever bear his hatred?

He turned his face toward her and smiled. "A penny for your thoughts."

She laughed lightly. "They're not worth a penny. I was just thinking of how peaceful and still everything is without electricity, but I'm glad you're here with me; I don't think I'd like to be alone in the dark."

Cory laughed. "I take it you meant that as a compliment. I hope you'll continue to enjoy my company when the lights go back on. I'd hate to have to work in darkness just to keep our relationship on a friendly footing." He lifted himself from the chair and Samantha saw in the moonlight that he was unbuttoning his shirt. "I hope you'll forgive me if I take off my shirt. I know it's not good manners, but this heat is really getting to me."

Samantha watched, fascinated. The rippling muscles of his masculine chest glistened in the moonlit darkness. She closed her eyes against the view, not trusting the desire that was burning in her heart. "I'm going to try to get some rest," she said, taking off her glasses. "There's no telling how long this blackout is going to last."

Samantha's body was as tense as a coiled spring. She pressed herself against the lounge chair, willing her rigid limbs to relax into the mindless safety of slumber. She knew Cory was watching her in the darkness and felt the searing intensity of his gaze burning through her shuttered eyelids, but she dared not open them for fear of the emotional surge that direct visual contact would bring.

She heard a sigh and a rustle and realized that Cory had turned away from her. Soon the deep even sound of his breathing indicated that he had fallen asleep. Somehow, the rhythm of Cory's subdued breathing, rising and falling in the darkness, relaxed Samantha and before long she found herself immersed in a restless slumber, well punctuated by the intermittent appearance of Cory's aquiline features.

Suddenly her fitful dreams became reality and Samantha awakened to find sunlight streaming down and Cory standing over her, an angry look on his face. He bent over her and lifted something from the side of the lounge chair. Samantha looked up, panic-stricken. He was holding the artificial nose bump in his hand.

"Would you care to explain this?" He reached down and rubbed his palm roughly across her cheek. "And your skin seems to be very clear today." The anger was building in his face and in his voice. He lowered himself and sat at the edge of the chaise, putting his hand behind the nape of her neck and pulling her toward him.

Savagely, his hands went to the bun behind her head and released the pins from her hair, causing it to fall freely in a wild frenzy about her shoulders. His face was so close that she could hear his rapid breathing.

"My, my, Miss Lorrimer, you're really quite attractive. Except for those unbecoming clothes, I would say you were a beautiful young woman." His hand reached toward the buttons on her blouse. "Perhaps these clothes are part of the act. I wonder what charms lie hidden behind these frumpy outfits?" Slowly, he began loosening the unopened lower buttons of the blouse.

Samantha gasped. "No! You mustn't." She pulled the top of her blouse together and jumped off the chair, moving away from Cory like a frightened animal.

His eyes raked her body viciously and he sneered disdainfully. "You'd better have an explanation for this . . . and make it a good one!" He began walking toward her.

She backed into the living room. "I don't have to explain anything to you. You wouldn't believe me anyway." Her eyes shot daggers at him. "I'm leaving. You can send my wages to my home. I hope you have better luck with your next secretary. Maybe you'll finally find a paragon to equal your precious Mrs. Harrison."

She bent, picked up her jacket, and reached for her bag, but before her fingers could close around it, Cory's hand grasped her wrist and turned her violently toward him.

"You're not going anywhere—not until I say so." He pulled her against him and she felt a throbbing rage move through his muscles. "You started this game, but I'm going to finish it—my way." His head dipped, and his lips met hers with an intensity that Samantha had never imagined possible. At first she struggled and tried to free herself, but his arms bound her to him like inflexible steel bands; the palm of one hand rested firmly on her back, and the other caressed the curve of her hip. She had no room to breathe, certainly no way to escape.

The pressure of his mouth against hers became more demanding, and she felt the tip of his tongue searching, probing, seeking unity with hers. All the hopeless yearning she had previously felt for Cory was reduced to one passionate moment, one abandoned response. She parted her lips, sharing and tasting a sweetness that was beyond anything she had ever experienced.

Cory was in complete control of the situation; all she wanted to do was please him. She moved closer, fitting the soft curves of her body to the hard length of his. Her fervent reaction seemed to increase the rigid tension within him; he lifted his head and moved his lips to the arching pulse of her neck.

"I've met scheming females before, but never one with your deceptive dedication. You're completely without morals, aren't you?" His lips were still pressed against her skin, his warm breath inflaming her flesh, and his whispered words came to her as if in a dream. "What did you hope to gain by this gruesome little charade? Did you think I would become totally dependent on you? That's it, isn't it? You intended to make yourself indispensable around the office, then, when the time was right, you'd reveal your true identity. You knew I'd find you physically attractive; you thought your charms would make me need you after office hours, as well."

His lips were soft against hers, but his voice was tight, low and cruel. "Fine, this is the perfect time to begin. Think of it as an audition. Let's see if you're as skilled at making love as you are at taking dictation." His hand moved down Samantha's back and slipped beneath the waistband of her skirt.

Cory's harsh words had turned Samantha's romantic reverie into an ugly nightmare. She suddenly realized, with a sinking feeling, that she loved him, and that she had foolishly persuaded herself that his embrace was a reciprocation of that love. In reality it was hate—ugly, vicious hate. He had turned what she felt for him into something sordid and horrible. She had to get away from him before she collapsed completely—either from the violence of his animosity or from shame at her own ardent response to his touch.

"You can't keep me here! You have no right."

Cory laughed, but there was no humor in his voice. "You're hardly in a position to talk about rights." He stepped back, and moving her hands between them, lifted them to his view. "Soft young hands—" his fingers cupped her chin— "sapphire eyes—" they combed through her hair —"hair like golden silk." His eyes were cold with hate as they devoured her body. "Don't talk to me about rights. I'll decide what my rights are, and you can be sure they won't include anything I've ever done with Mrs. Harrison."

His hand moved over her body—slowly—intimately—carefully discovering each curvaceous detail she had sought to hide.

"How you must have been laughing at me. Carson knew, didn't he? Pygmalion indeed! Well I'm the one who's going to see this transformation; Carson can just keep on wondering." His hand went to the collar of her blouse.

His ugly threat sent Samantha into a paroxysm of fear, and lifting her foot, she delivered a sharp kick against his left shin.

"You witch," he hissed, rubbing his hand against his injured leg. "You'll pay for that."

But Samantha had no intention of hanging around; the instant he released her she grabbed her tote bag from the coffee table and fled to the stairway. Hot tears of shame and remorse flooded her face and blurred her vision as she ran down the many flights of stairs and arrived at the street without even realizing how she had gotten there.

Somehow she survived the long bus ride to Greenwich Village, let herself into the apartment and collapsed on the sofa, crying desperately into her folded hands. Janet came drifting sleepily out of the bedroom, concern showing in her dreamy black eyes.

"What's happened? I knew you were caught in the blackout, but I assumed you were all right. I just tried to call your office but the phone lines were overloaded."

Samantha panted, trying to catch her breath and collect her emotions. She waved her arm in front of her face and spoke in a ragged voice. "It's nothing . . . I'm fine . . . I spent the night at Cory's apartment."

Janet lifted her eyebrows and sat down, pausing to light a cigarette. "You spent the night with Cory Talbott? What happened to your high moral code?"

Samantha shook her head disconsolately. "No, it's nothing like that. Cory invited me to dinner and then he was going to help me with some of my schoolwork. His girlfriend is out of town, so he thought this would be a convenient occasion. As for seducing me, nothing could be further from the man's mind. Any designs he has on my body stem from a vicious desire for revenge." Once more she broke into uncontrollable tears.

"Samantha, whatever are you talking about? I thought Cory was pleased with your work. You said everything was going along so well."

"It was—until this morning. Then Cory discovered what I was doing and . . . oh, Janet . . . if you could have seen the disgust in his eyes."

"Didn't you explain things to him? Couldn't he understand why you were forced to do such a thing? You yourself admitted that you never would have gotten the job without the help of the disguise."

"He didn't give me a chance to explain anything. He was vicious, Janet. I told him I was quitting and he could send me my wages. I don't think I could ever bear to look at him again."

Janet came over and placed her hand on her shoulder. "Well, for someone who wants to lead a quiet, uneventful life, you certainly do have an interesting way of creating your own excitement. But don't worry about anything. Remember, Jim said he would use his contacts to find a job for you if you ever needed one. Everything will work out. Why don't you take a warm bath and curl up in bed? You don't have to go in to work today and I have some script changes to study so we can take the phone off the hook and relax."

It was late afternoon before Samantha came awake. She gazed vacantly at the ceiling, feeling trapped by her own thoughts. She might well be able to escape the violence of Cory's wrath, but how could she ever find relief from her own bitter feelings of shame about what she had done? Sighing deeply, she slid her feet to the floor and rose from the bed. She went into the bathroom and washed her face, noticing that her skin really had returned to its own honey-toned clarity.

Janet heard her moving about and entered the room just as Samantha was looking through her wardrobe, trying to decide what to wear.

"Here, wear something sexy. That always makes me feel better. It should help you recover from all those horrible outfits you've been wearing lately."

Samantha grasped the silk lounging pajamas Janet had offered and began to change into them. "Maybe you're right. Maybe if I look better outside, I'll begin to feel better inside." She adjusted the tie that fastened the belt of the outfit and ran her hand along the low vee of the neckline to straighten it out. Then she slipped her feet into a pair of soft kid wedge-heeled slippers and began to brush her hair so it fell softly about her face. She applied a light rosy blusher and the slightest touch of blue eye shadow. She turned and swirled before Janet, letting the wide pants flare around her legs. "How do I look?"

"A lot better than you've looked in a long time. In a way I'm glad Cory found out about your deception. It was absolutely ridiculous for you to go about in such a horrid disguise. I don't know how I could have ever thought of such a wild idea." She led the way to the kitchen, where she picked up a bottle of chilled white wine and two thin-stemmed glasses.

"Janet, it's only five o'clock. It's too early to start having wine. We're not part of the jet set, you know."

"I know, but I'd like to celebrate the return of my roommate and friend. I didn't like rooming with old Miss Frump. I'd hate to think of you becoming as mean and heartless as Cory Talbott."

Samantha's eyes softened with hidden pain. "He's not always mean and heartless. You should see the way Denise Gerard twists him around her little manicured finger. He's just like a little boy around her. I guess he doesn't mind a touch of beauty in his private life; it's just in his office that he expects everyone to function like a bunch of heartless machines. Maybe you're right; maybe I am better off being out of there, but it did seem like such a golden opportunity."

The doorbell rang and Samantha motioned for Janet to remain seated. "I've been sleeping all afternoon; now you just rest and enjoy your wine. I'll take care of everything." She walked to the door, holding her wineglass, and opened it.

Her heart leaped wildly and her breath caught in her throat as she stared up at Cory Talbott. "What do you want?"

Cory didn't answer her. He pushed his way into the apartment and looked coldly at Janet, who was still seated on the couch, then turned back to face Samantha, who leaned weakly against the door. "I came here to see if we could straighten out this situation. I told the office you were home resting from the aftereffects of the blackout." An ugly snort escaped his tight lips. "I had no idea I'd find you celebrating the marvelous success your little masquerade has had."

Janet slipped off the couch. "Just a minute there, Mr. High and Mighty."

Cory eyed her coldly. "This is a private matter, and I'd appreciate some privacy."

Janet looked at Samantha. Samantha nodded, and Janet began walking toward the bedroom. She opened the door and looked over her shoulder at Samantha. "Yell if you need me." Then she closed the door, leaving behind an atmosphere of frigid hostility.

Cory came toward Samantha and grasped her by the shoulders. His eyes wandered over her face and down her body. It was as if he were seeing her for the first time and wanted to commit each minute detail to memory. She felt him mentally removing her garments, piece by piece.

"What a sly little witch you turned out to be." Cory's voice was taut with anger. He tightened his grip, and his fingers bit into her shoulder. "I hope you had a good laugh, because I feel like choking that smile off your face." Pushing her away from him, he released her, and shoved his hands into his pockets as if he didn't trust himself to touch her.

"No wonder you forgot the background information you listed on your employment application—everything you said was just one big lie." He shook his head in disbelief. "You've made me look like an utter fool. I've met cold women before, but none of them ever approached your level of calculated deception. Look at you—liquor in hand—not an iota of remorse. You're unbelievable!"

Samantha put the glass on the table and her voice was a shaky whisper. "For your information, I wasn't celebrating the success of my masquerade. As a matter of fact, it was a dismal failure. I've never been so sorry about anything in my life."

Cory turned and glared at her. "I'll just bet!" His eyes continued cutting into her body, then wavered, as if he were momentarily undecided. "Then why did you do it? And why me?"

Samantha put her hands over her face and began to cry. "I wanted a job—I wanted one so much, I thought I could do anything. But I was wrong. I'm so sorry." Her sobs grew louder.

Cory moved closer; his voice was soft. "O.K. You needed a job—but why the disguise?"

Samantha bit her lower lip and held back her tears. Traces of anger still hardened his eyes, but there was a softening of his features that made Samantha want to throw herself in his arms and beg for his forgiveness. She forced herself to speak. "Look at me. Would I have been hired as your secretary? No; admit it, I never would have gotten past Mrs. Harrison's nose. Do you really want to know why I wore a disguise?" She drew a deep breath, threw back her shoulders, and walked up to him. "Do you actually think I just wanted to play a trick on the famous Cory Talbott? Don't flatter yourself. I just wanted a good job so I could learn the investment field. But every employer treated me like an empty-headed little tart and tried to make me into his back-office sweetie. Now do you understand?"

Cory's eyes glinted ominously, two cold chips of steel. "Perhaps I have been unfair to you, but"—his lips curled in a disdainful sneer— "you must admit that you misjudged me. Why didn't you tell me the truth at once? I certainly had no designs on your body. Surely you don't think that I would make any romantic overtures to someone who wouldn't welcome them . . . least of all my secretary. You, too, flatter yourself, Miss Lorrimer. Your charms are not so powerful that I find them irresistible, although I did momentarily lose control this morning." He shook his head as if he were annoyed with himself. "I'm here to apologize and promise that it won't happen again."

Savagely shrugging his shoulders, he turned to look at her. "In any case, now that we've settled the confusion, there's no reason why we can't go back to our previous working arrangement. I have no desire to lose a good secretary and you must be happy to find an employer whose morals, toward you at least, are above reproach. So, I'll expect you in the office tomorrow morning at your usual time."

Samantha gasped and groped her way to her seat, hoping her weak, spaghetti limbs would reach the chair before she collapsed. "I can't," she said, shaking her head wildly, causing the velvety smoothness of her hair to cascade tempestuously about her face. "How could we work together after everything that's happened? It's just impossible."

Cory reached down and drew her out of the chair. The hint of compassion she had seen before seemed to have vanished. His icy eyes cut into her and froze her heart, taking her breath away. He pulled her into his arms, startling her with the sudden force of his actions. A malicious smile curved the corner of his mouth, and before she could recover her senses, his lips had imprisoned hers.

This kiss held none of the ferocious anger she had felt that morning. Instead of demanding, Cory was coaxing, gently moving his lips against hers, seducing her with the potency of his caress. His hand traveled slowly down her back; his probing fingers sent icy shivers along the ridges of her spine.

All of Samantha's powers of coherent reasoning vanished; her only awareness was of Cory and the uncharted fields of ecstasy he was urging her to explore. Her arms came up, and her hands curled around his neck, pulling him closer, telling him how much she loved him.

Her lips willingly parted in response to the persuasion of his and her body pressed hungrily against him, savoring the intimacy of his embrace. Her mind no'longer controlled the movements of her body as she yielded fully to the erotic power of the emotions that Cory's touch had unleashed.

Then suddenly he lifted his head and set her away from him. She felt chilled—deserted—and she tried to move closer, to feel once more the strength of his body pressing against hers. Her eyes pleaded with him to again enclose her in the security of his arms, because she now knew that she could never be happy anywhere else.

Cory met her plaintive gaze with eyes that were cold and aloof; he seemed totally unmoved by the experience they had just shared. He was obviously in full control of all his emotions as he studied the confusion on Samantha's face. His cynically triumphant smile stabbed her heart, smothering the joyful fires he had ignited only moments ago, and she couldn't believe the chilling calm of his voice.

"As you can see, there's no reason for you to worry about me losing my head over you. Of course, if you're worried about your own lack of control . . ." He smiled knowingly at her before continuing. "I have no need to force my attentions on a woman who merely wants a chance to work—as you so fervently claim. There are still a lot of things about the securities industry which you *can* learn from me—so if you're really serious, we'll begin your education right now.

"The first lesson you must learn about the world of high finance is never to panic, no matter how stressful the situation. Your behavior at my apartment this morning was typical of a flighty female, not at all what one would expect of a clearheaded financial executive. You'll certainly have to become less emotional if you expect to achieve any measure of success in the investment industry. The next thing you must learn is that I never take no for an answer. I promise you that your feminine attractions, such as they may be," he said, his eyes raking her body in a condescending manner, "are perfectly safe with me. If you don't take me at my word, I'll assume that everything you've told me is untrue and I'll see to it that you never get another position of any consequence in the investment industry. So unless you intend to return to your father's dairy farm, I suggest you reconsider your decision." He tilted his head and tightened his grip on her arms.

She lowered her head, no longer able to look into his eyes. "All right, you make yourself perfectly clear. I don't think it's a good idea and I know you'll never trust me again, but I suppose we can give it a try."

Cory loosened his grip on Samantha's arm. "A very wise decision, Miss Lorrimer." He walked to the door and let his eyes travel over the revealing curves, scarcely hidden by the clinging cloth of her pajama suit. "While you may not choose to wear anything as unattractive as the outfits you've been coming to work in, I suggest you wear something a bit more conservative than what you have on now. Although I have no designs on your physical charms, the other men in the office may not be so immune." He smiled wickedly and closed the door behind him.

Chapter Five

The next morning Samantha selected her clothing with great care. Cory Talbott's parting words still rang in her ears and she wanted to show him that she could dress in proper business attire without assuming an unattractive disguise. She chose a cool high-collared white cotton blouse that buttoned down the front, a calf-length madras skirt and a pair of plain low-heeled pumps that downplayed the shapely length of her legs.

She smoothed her skirt and studied her reflection in the full-length mirror on the closet door. Her outfit was probably as simple as any of those she had previously worn, but the flattering fit, which stressed the striking contours of her body, made it look infinitely more attractive.

She brushed her silky blond hair to the back of her head, gathering it up in the same severe bun she had always worn to the office, and considered applying a light touch of makeup, but decided against it.

She saw her horn-rimmed glasses lying on the dressing table and placed them on the bridge of her nose, hoping they might provide an additional shield against the prying eyes she was sure to encounter at the office.

She knew that the real challenge would come from Mrs. Harrison and she wondered if the older woman would try to pressure her into quitting her job. Then she would be neatly trapped between Mrs. Harrison's hostility and Cory's ultimatum. She knew that Cory was probably only too eager to have her out of his office, but she also knew that his strong male ego made it necessary for him to keep her on until he had exacted his full measure of vengeance.

Cory had apparently been at the office the previous day because there was a full tape in Samantha's dictating machine, indicating he had left some work for her to do. She placed the earphones around her head, and the clear, impersonal sounds of Cory's voice came to her through the machine. She began typing the letters he had dictated.

At ten o'clock the door swung briskly open and Samantha knew who it was without even looking up. In a matter of seconds Cory covered the distance from the door to her desk and switched off her dictating machine. She removed her earphones and looked up warily.

He studied her face for a moment before speaking, then said, "Please come into my office, Miss Lorrimer, and close the door behind you."

Samantha paused to pick up her steno pad and several sharp pencils before following him into the office. She closed the door and waited for him to sit down so she could settle herself in her chair and begin taking dictation. But instead of seating himself behind his desk, he came toward her, his eyes openly raking her body in shameless appraisal. She felt a heated flush rise through her as he folded his arms across his broad chest and walked slowly around her. Her fists clenched both pencils and pad tightly as she lowered her eyes to the carpet. This was a situation for which she was totally unprepared and she didn't know how to react to it. Finally she had had enough. "Are you quite through with your examination? Do I meet with your approval? If not I shall be only too happy to leave this office."

Cory tilted his head and curved his lips in an arrogantly amused smile. His gray eyes narrowed with careless disdain. "Why would I want you to leave? It seems I hardly know you, although there is something vaguely familiar about you. I get the feeling that we've met before, but I can't place where." He stood back, as if he wanted to get a clearer view of her by putting some distance between them. "You are a most intriguing woman. First you appear to be quite unattractive—a withered old maid, one might say—then yesterday, at your apartment, you looked quite the part of a femme fatale and now, this morning, you appear to be every inch the handsomely efficient young businesswoman. I hardly know what to make of it."

"Why make anything of it?" Samantha said coldly. "You told me I was to dress properly for the office and I was merely trying to comply with your directive. I sincerely hope you're pleased with my appearance."

Cory lifted his head and a twinkle replaced the steel in his gray eyes. He let them wander slowly over her body, intimately viewing and evaluating every sensuous curve. "But, Miss Lorrimer, you're sadly mistaken. I quite approved of your appearance last evening. I only pointed out that your attire might be inappropriate for the office. After all, you must admit that your outfit was hardly what a liberated young businesswoman would wear. I would say it was more suggestive of a sultan's harem. Now this ensemble conceals quite a bit of what was revealed yesterday. Except for the fact that I have an excellent memory, I might be hesitant to believe what sultry charms lie hidden beneath that pure white blouse." He walked toward her, letting his eyes travel slowly over her quivering form. "You have definite possibilities, Miss Lorrimer, and I believe you'll be even more of an asset to our company than I had previously thought."

Samantha threw her pad and pencils down on his desk. The fire that had been burning in her cheeks was now flaming in her eyes. "Just a minute! You know all about my deception now, so don't think you can make me feel guilty about that. I admit it was a mistake, but I offered to leave the job. You were the one who insisted we could go on working together, claiming your morals were above reproach. Well, don't imagine you can go around evaluating me as if I were some slave up for auction. This won't be the first job I've had to leave because of a lecherous employer."

Cory's eyes darkened and his mouth tightened in derisive anger. "Don't flatter yourself, Miss Lorrimer. You have no cause to accuse me of any indecent intentions toward your body. I was merely trying to accustom myself to your new image. You must admit, it is quite a change from your previous appearance. Let me further remind you that, since I have no romantic designs on your anatomy, I have no need to let you behave in a manner which does not befit any other employee of this company. As you are well aware, I'm not in the habit of tolerating emotional outbursts. I'll excuse you this time, since I realize you're still feeling guilty about your failed scheme; however, I won't be so magnanimous in the future. Have I made myself perfectly clear?" He stood looking down at Samantha, the chill in his withering gaze almost palpable.

Samantha's insides were a steaming cauldron. She opened her mouth, about to let loose, when she looked straight into his unyielding eyes. She remembered his contemptuous vow to see that she would never get another job in the securities industry, and one glance at his determined expression convinced her that he was not in the habit of making empty threats. She swallowed her pride, tasting the evil bile of defeat as it slowly slid down her throat. "Yes, Mr. Talbott. You've made yourself perfectly clear. I apologize for my behavior and promise that it won't happen again."

The triumphant gleam of victory glistened in Cory's eyes. "That's more like it, Miss Lorrimer. Now perhaps we can get down to the business of this office, which, I believe, is managing our clients' investments." He settled himself comfortably behind his desk. "I have some correspondence I would like to dictate. Would you please retrieve your pad and pencil so that we can begin?"

Cory dictated to her in the same rapid-fire manner in which he did his thinking, and before long Samantha found herself forgetting her anger and becoming totally engrossed in the work at hand. She had turned to a clean page and was poised for the next letter when Cory said, "I believe that should do it for now, Miss Lorrimer. Do you think you could get me a cup of coffee and then see to those letters? I'd like them to go out today."

Samantha rose from her chair and answered Cory in carefully measured tones. "I have no intention of leaving until all my work is completed, Mr. Talbott. And I'll get your coffee immediately."

She left his private office, dropped the steno pad and pencils on her desk and went to the coffee machine. While she was at the machine, her back to the door, Billy entered with the morning mail.

"Good morning, Samantha. I was sorry to hear you were out sick yesterday."

Samantha turned to face Billy. She was about to speak but she froze when she saw Billy's startled face. His mouth was hanging open and his eyes were riveted on her newly revealed figure.

"Samantha, is that really you? What happened? I never would have recognized you."

Cory strode through the doorway and angrily took the hot coffee from Samantha's quivering hand. "Here, you'd better let me have that before you wind up with a bad burn." Then he turned to Billy. "O.K., Billy. Close your mouth and unglue your feet. No doubt you've noticed the change in Miss Lorrimer's appearance; however, I do not intend for her to be subjected to any intrusive questioning about her private life. Therefore, I expect no further discussion will be accorded the matter. Since I understand that you are on close speaking terms with most of the personnel in this office, I hope you will take it upon yourself to make my desires known to the rest of the staff. There is to be no further discussion about the change in Miss Lorrimer's appearance and I will be most displeased if anyone chooses to disregard this directive. Do I make myself perfectly clear?"

Billy straightened his shoulders and headed for the door. "Yes, Mr. Talbott. I'll see to it right away."

Cory shot a wordlessly cold glance in Samantha's direction, then took his coffee and entered his office, closing the door behind him.

The rest of the morning passed quickly. Cory was on the phone constantly and Samantha was occupied with typing the correspondence he had dictated. Once again, Cory instructed her to send out for sandwiches and they ate at their desks. Samantha was happy about the fact that, since the older woman was on vacation for three weeks, she had not had to face Mrs. Harrison. And apparently Billy had done an excellent job of spreading the news about her altered appearance because, with the exception of a few stealthy glances, no attention was paid to it.

She completed the correspondence and brought it in to Cory for his signature. He was seated at his desk, charting some numbers on a graph, and didn't look up as she entered, but motioned her to a chair beside his desk. "I'll be with you in a moment. I've been following these marine bonds for several months and I think we may be approaching a buy signal." Then he entered a small x on a numbered portion of the graph and threw his pencil down. "There it is, Miss Lorrimer. If these bonds go down tomorrow, we're going to buy them for several of our clients. I've been on the phone all day lining up purchasers and we should have quite a busy day tomorrow."

Samantha looked over at the chart on his desk. Her eyes narrowed as she vainly tried to comprehend what he was saying. His talk about alphas and betas might have been a discussion of the

Greek alphabet rather than some important investment tool.

Cory noticed both her frown and her apparent interest in what he was doing. "Haven't they taught you about alpha and beta curves at that school you're attending?" He snorted derisively when Samantha shook her head. "That's one of the most important theories of modern investment. How do they expect you to learn anything if you don't know the basics? You'll learn more in a few weeks in this office than you'll ever learn there!" He motioned her toward the desk. "Come over here and let me explain this to you. You'll never be able to do anything if you don't understand this."

Samantha placed the letters on the corner of Cory's desk and walked around to where he was seated. He moved his chair back, making room for her, then moved it forward, trapping Samantha between himself and the desk. He seemed totally oblivious to her discomfort and leaned intently over the chart, tracing a carefully drawn line of x marks with one lean brown finger. "This is when we first started the chart, several months ago," he said, pointing to an x on the chart. "This is the price, based on past performance of the stock, at which it becomes a profitable purchase, and this is what the stock is selling for today. Now do you understand why I'm so excited about its price level?"

He shifted his chair to get a bulging folder from his drawer. When he moved back to the desk he placed his arm around the far side of

Samantha rather than between the two of them. Now she was forced to move closer to him to avoid the touch of his casually encircling arm. The spicy scent of his cologne drifted enticingly toward her quivering nostrils and she felt her legs growing shaky beneath her, but there was no way she could free herself without arousing Cory's suspicions, and that was the last thing she wanted to do. She bit her lip and forced herself to concentrate on what he was saying.

His voice was calm and businesslike; he was apparently totally unaware of the tension he was creating in Samantha. He was intent on his explanation, and Samantha might have been a callow young boy for all the amorous excitement she was generating in him. His voice droned on.

"These charts show the price movements of the stock over the past ten years. Now you can see how closely our latest chart is paralleling the previous years." His arm tightened around her waist and he pulled her closer, trying to give her a better view of the charts spread out on his desk. Then he turned his head and looked up into her eyes. "There, is that clear now? Do you understand what I've been saying? Tomorrow you'll get a chance to see how we put it all into practice. It promises to be a long and interesting day." Suddenly he became aware of Samantha's precarious position and moved his chair back, leaving her free to return to her seat at the side of the desk. He leaned back in his chair, twisting a pencil thoughtfully in his hands, and narrowed his eyes in Samantha's direction.

"You haven't heard a word I've said, have you? Really, Miss Lorrimer, you shock me. First you claim that you want to be accorded the same treatment as a man and when I do just that, you turn into a blushing Victorian maiden. You'll really have to curb your wild imagination if you hope to get ahead in the investment industry. Please try to remember that we are in a business office, not a bedroom, and channel your thoughts accordingly. Now, what did you want to see me about before we got off on this tangent?"

Samantha handed him the letters. "You wanted these to go out today, but I think we're too late for the mail room," she said, glancing at the digital clock on Cory's desk. "It's six o'clock and they usually leave at five-thirty. My lesson took longer than one might have expected. However, since it's my fault the letters didn't reach the mail room in time, I'll drop them off at the post office on my way home."

When Cory didn't answer her, but began signing the letters immediately, Samantha left the room, closing the door behind her. She had completed most of her work and there was very little for her to do as she waited for Cory to finish. She went to drop something off on Mrs. Harrison's desk and when she returned to her office Cory was half seated on the edge of the desk, holding a pile of envelopes in his hand.

"All the letters were done perfectly, so I sealed them up. However, I can't find where you've hidden the stamps. I never was much good at understanding the intricacies of my secretary's office—if you'll just find the stamps and place them on the envelopes, we can be on our way."

Samantha quickly found the stamps and began to attach them to the letters. Without lifting her eyes she spoke to Cory. "There's no need for you to wait, Mr. Talbott. I'll be finished in a few minutes."

"It's no bother. I can wait; I have no pressing engagements this evening. The rest of the office is empty and I wouldn't feel right about leaving you here alone."

Samantha bristled. "I'm a big girl, Mr. Talbott, and I'm perfectly capable of taking care of myself."

Cory let his gaze travel meaningfully over Samantha's body. "It's very obvious that you're a big girl; there's no disputing that, but as to whether you're able to take care of yourself—*that* remains to be seen." An arrogant grin covered his face as Samantha's hands began to shake at his open mockery.

She stamped the remainder of the envelopes with more force than was necessary, wishing they were Cory's tauntingly arrogant features instead. But her anger only seemed to amuse him more and she completed her task with a decisive bang. Then, taking up her handbag and the stamped envelopes, she headed for the door. "Good night, Mr. Talbott. Thank you for staying and protecting me from all those unbelievably threatening dangers." She flung the door open and hurried through it, only to have it caught by Cory before it could close. He waited silently with her by the elevator. When it arrived he gently but firmly lowered Samantha's hand as it reached for the lobby button and pressed the garage level.

Samantha pulled a face. "I need the lobby, not the garage. I don't happen to own a car."

Cory smiled gently. "But I do, and I can drive you to the post office. It's not out of my way. After all, it is my mail you're taking."

Samantha bristled and reached for the controls once more. "It may be your mail, but it's my responsibility to see that it gets taken care of. Please let me go. I'd much rather walk."

Cory stilled her hand once more. "Ah, but I insist, and I am the boss."

Samantha had no answer for that and the ride continued in silence until they reached the garage. Cory steered Samantha toward the Jaguar and the trip to the post office was completed without conversation. Cory moved into a parking spot and clasped his muscular hand over Samantha's handbag as she opened the car door. She reached for it, looking at him quizzically when he tightened his grip, indicating that he was not about to release it.

During the short trip from the office, the tension in Samantha had risen to a feverish pitch and she carefully controlled her breathing in an attempt to keep the distress from showing in her voice. "May I please have my handbag?"

Cory was totally unruffled by her request. "Why? Don't you trust me?"

Samantha was exasperated. Her voice came out in a high-pitched shriek that approached hysteria. "Of course I trust you. What has that got to do with it? I want my handbag. It's mine and I need it. I don't understand the point of this ridiculous discussion."

Cool gray eyes calmly surveyed her. "I agree with you wholeheartedly. This entire conversation is an inane waste of time. There's certainly no reason for you to think that I have any use for your handbag or its contents. I'll just keep it here until you return from the post office. After all, the letters are all stamped and ready to mail—there's absolutely no need for you to take your handbag with you."

"But I'm not returning to the car. I'm going right home after I mail these letters."

"Fine, you'll mail the letters and then I'll drive you home. It's not at all out of my way. Your handbag will be waiting for you, safely in my care, when you return to the car. Now, why don't you get moving so we don't waste any more of that valuable time we were just discussing?"

Samantha pursed her lips in anger and exhaled violently as she slammed the car door and strode sullenly toward the post office. It took her only a few minutes to post the letters, since she had already divided them into local and out-of-town categories. She placed each packet in the correct slot and returned to the car. The short sojourn hadn't improved her temper and she flung herself into the car, slammed the door shut and sat staring sulkily off into space through the wide expanse of the windshield.

Cory started up the engine and turned to look

at her, a patronizing grin covering his face. "Where would you like to eat?"

Samantha gritted her teeth, still staring straight ahead. "I would like to go home."

Totally unperturbed, Cory looked away from Samantha as he deftly rejoined the flowing stream of traffic. "Well then, home you shall go. Your slightest wish is my command."

The car moved slowly through the early evening traffic with Cory whistling calmly to himself while Samantha continued to stare sullenly out the window, pressing herself as far away from his seat as possible. It was obvious to her that Cory was determined to make every aspect of her existence totally miserable. There was absolutely no reason for his behavior tonight except that he had wanted to ruin her evening.

Well, his mission had been successfully accomplished. Now she would spend the remainder of the evening seething with unspent anger while he would celebrate his intimidation of her.

The most upsetting part about the whole thing was that there was nothing Samantha could do about it. There was absolutely no doubt in her mind that he was deadly serious when he said he would ruin her career if she tried to resign from her job. He intended to make her pay dearly for her little masquerade.

The car came to a halt by the curb and Samantha prepared to leave. However, as she reached for the door handle she realized that they were not at her Greenwich Village apartment. Instead, they were in that downtown section of lower Manhattan known as Little Italy because of its many Italian residents.

The area abounded with sausage and cheese stores, wine shops, pastry shops and small gourmet shops crammed with unique Italian delicacies. The car had halted in front of one of the most famous of these gourmet shops.

Samantha turned to Cory and opened her mouth, ready to question his actions, but he only smiled and patted her hand gently. "I'll just be a minute," he said as he removed the car keys and opened his door. "Stay put; I'll be right back." Flashing the beguiling smile that still could make Samantha's heart turn over, he disappeared into the shop.

Samantha drummed her fingers impatiently. She wanted to leave the car and go home right now. There was no need to wait to be driven. She was only a few short blocks from home and she was certainly capable of walking that small distance without any difficulty. She considered what Cory's reaction would be the following morning and decided to chance it. His only weapon against her was his power to make her uncomfortable. She just wouldn't let him force her into leaving her job and ruining her entire career. He didn't know just how determined she was to make something of herself. Sooner or later, when he saw that his punitive actions were getting him nowhere, he would tire of the game and let her go.

She opened the door and scrambled out of the car, walking rapidly until she turned the corner and disappeared from view. When she reached it the apartment was empty, and when she walked into the bedroom to change her clothes, she found a note from Janet leaning on her vanity mirror.

Have gone to rehearse lines and have dinner with Jim. Leftover stew in refrigerator. See you later.

Janet

Samantha wrinkled her nose. Leftover stew. The thought was terribly unappealing. Maybe she would forego dinner. In any case, the first order of business was to lounge in a warm bath and let the tension generated by Mr. Cory Talbott disappear down the drain.

She had just settled herself to the point where she could close her eyes and relax when the doorbell rang. Darn, she thought. Why is it whenever you get into the bath, either the doorbell or the telephone rings? Well, I'm not expecting anyone, so whoever it is can just go away and come back later.

But the ringing didn't stop, and it was almost as if someone had decided to lean on the bell until it was answered. Samantha uttered a mild oath and wrapped herself in a large bath towel, not bothering to dry herself. She had no intention of opening the door, and as soon as she got rid of whoever it was out there she intended to return to the soothing comfort of her tub.

"Who is it?" she said, speaking to the solid wall of the door.

"It's me; Cory. Will you please open the door?"

Samantha's heart began to pound wildly. He had followed her home. She hadn't considered that she might have to face the full force of his wrath before morning. Her nerves began to jangle as she tried to think of a way out. "What do you want?"

"I want to come in. Open the door!"

"You can't come in; I'm taking a bath."

"I don't care what you're doing. I'm carrying a heavy package and I want to get inside and put it down. Now, will you stop behaving like a spoiled child and open this door?"

Cory's implication that she was not mature enough to deal with the situation only made Samantha angrier. Tucking the towel securely above her breasts, she removed the chain and flung the door open. "Come on in. Make yourself at home, but don't expect me to entertain you!"

Without waiting for Cory's reaction, she flounced into her bedroom, locking the door behind her. Then the irony of the situation hit her. Cory was making her a prisoner in her own home and she had no intention of spending the rest of the evening locked up in her bedroom just because he had decided to take control of the rest of her apartment.

Throwing the towel on the bed, she slipped into her underthings. Then she put on a pair of old jeans and a tee shirt. It was her home and neither Cory Talbott nor anyone else was going to make her feel uncomfortable in it. Straightening her shoulders, she walked out of the bedroom.

Cory was busy emptying a huge bag of groceries onto the kitchen counter. He looked up as she came in, sweeping her with a coldly appraising stare. "I see you changed for dinner. You didn't have to, you know. The towel was quite becoming."

Samantha looked angrily at him. "What are you doing here?"

"What does it look like I'm doing? I'm preparing dinner—something I might have expected you to be doing, since you *did* invite me here."

Samantha gripped the table and looked over at him, staring incredulously into his face. "I *invited* you here? Are you insane? I never did any such thing."

Cory looked at her as if he were dealing with some mentally incapacitated individual and sighed with exasperation. "I declare, Miss Lorrimer, I do believe you're losing your memory. I asked you where you would like to have dinner and you insisted upon going home. I was perfectly willing to take you to one of New York's finer dining places, but as you know, I always try to please, so I stopped off on the way and picked up a sumptuous assortment of Italian delicacies. When I returned to the car, I found you gone. Naturally, I assumed you had run home to prepare the table and get things ready for our dinner. Imagine my surprise when I found you lounging in the bath, expecting me to do all the work. I genuinely believe the old Miss Lorrimer was much more efficient." There was a teasing sparkle in his eyes as he spoke but Samantha was in no mood to notice it.

"How dare you say that about me? I've never

been lazy. My work is of the highest caliber and I always see that it's finished."

Cory settled himself on a chair beside the kitchen table and leaned back, folding his arms across the broad expanse of his chest. "Very well, if what you say is true, I expect you to act the part of a gracious hostess and start preparing the tasty dinner which I have so generously purchased. It's not at all courteous to make a dinner guest prepare his own meal, unless, of course, you had some predinner entertainment planned?" He looked meaningfully toward the bedroom. "I really wish you had kept on the towel. It's so much easier to take off."

Samantha glared at him and began storming around the kitchen, placing plates, napkins and silverware on the table. Then she unwrapped the plethora of packages Cory had purchased. "You happen to be an uninvited dinner guest," she said, speaking between clenched teeth.

"That's a highly debatable point," said Cory. "I was sure you were inviting me to dine at your home this evening and even if I was mistaken in my assumption, a gracious hostess would do everything possible to make her guest, invited or not, feel at home."

All right, Mr. Cory Talbott, Samantha thought, two can play at this little game of yours. I'm not the complete idiot you take me to be. I may not be the Wizard of Wall Street, but I'm certainly capable of giving you a good run for your money. "You're absolutely right, Mr. Talbott. I have been remiss in my duties as a hostess. I can't imagine what's gotten into me.

Now, you just sit there and I'll see to everything."

Her sarcasm seemed completely lost on Cory as he settled himself more comfortably in his chair. "That's more like it. Would you mind getting me the corkscrew so I can open this bottle of wine?" he said, fingering a raffia-covered flask of Chianti.

Samantha smiled despite herself and handed him the corkscrew, then she placed the wineglasses on the table. Cory rose from his seat and moved to the opposite side of the table, holding out her chair for her. She sat down and surveyed the food before her.

"You must have bought out the store. What are all these things?"

"Just my favorite Italian foods. I really enjoy a meal like this, which is one of the reasons I was so happy to hear you suggest eating at your place this evening." He blithely ignored Samantha's cutting glare and continued. "This is spiced eggplant, these are pickled mushrooms and these are hot red peppers. The meats and cheeses are too delightful to explain. Just try them first and then I'll tell you what they are."

Samantha sampled a little of everything and enjoyed it thoroughly. By the time the meal was finished, the wine had lifted her spirits and she was actually able to converse with Cory in an easy, friendly manner.

"I don't suppose you have any espresso in the house?" he said, breaking into Samantha's languid state.

She moved leisurely from her chair. "No,

sorry. Instant will have to do." She began spooning coffee crystals into the cups and set the water up to boil.

"Ugh," Cory said. "It's an absolute crime to eat Tony's delicious pastries with instant coffee. But I guess we'll have to make do with whatever's available."

Samantha cleared the table while the water was boiling, then took their dessert into the living room. Totally relaxed as a result of the wine and food, she kicked off her shoes and put her feet up on the couch. She had forgotten her earlier anger with Cory and was now completely at ease in his company.

He studied her with strangely soft eyes, his head tilted to one side. "Why don't you take your hair down? That ridiculous bun spoils the lovely picture of total tranquillity."

Samantha stretched languidly. "I'm too tired to move. Anyway, it's not bothering me."

Cory sprang lithely from his seat. "Well, it's bothering me, so I'll take it down."

Samantha tensed as he approached her. His hands went to the back of her head, deftly removing the pins, then slipping through her hair and lifting her face so that her eyes met his. She read his meaning and sat up in her seat, about to protest, when they both heard the sound of a key in the door. The door opened and Janet stepped into the room, closely followed by Jim Carson.

Janet looked at Cory as he stood leaning over Samantha. She raised one eyebrow delicately and spoke in her clear, honeyed voice. "I'm sorry if we're interrupting anything, but I didn't know you had company, Samantha."

Cory straightened quickly and withdrew his hand from the back of Samantha's neck. "We were late finishing up at the office and I suggested that we might enjoy some food from my favorite Italian grocery. We've just had our coffee and I was about to leave."

Jim settled himself comfortably in the rocking chair. "Don't leave on our account, Cory. I was planning on coming to see you tomorrow anyway. Maybe I can save myself a trip."

"No use, Jim. We have a busy day ahead of us tomorrow, so I have to be leaving. Give me a call in the morning and we can set up a lunch date later in the week."

He waved to Samantha and let himself out the door.

"Well," Janet said, "what was that all about?"

"You heard. We worked late and decided to have a quick bite for dinner. Now I've got to get to bed."

Samantha said good night and went into the bedroom, closing the door behind her. She moved slowly around the room, choosing her clothing for the following morning and hanging it carefully on her closet door. The muted tones of the conversation in the living room drifted through the closed door and she blushed, remembering the startled look on Janet's face when she entered the apartment. She couldn't help but wonder what turn events might have taken if Janet and Jim hadn't returned when they did.

She slid beneath the cool sheets of her bed and pulled the covers protectively over her, but nothing could keep her mind from turning to Cory's gentle manner of such a short time ago and from wishing that they hadn't been interrupted so soon.

Chapter Six

The next day at the office was as frenzied as Cory had said it would be, as were the days that followed. A number of issues that Cory had been tracking hit a buy level, and Samantha was kept busy recording the orders he executed. They skipped lunch frequently, and it was once again after six when he called her in on a Thursday a week later to say that they had completed their purchases and all she had to do was register them with the back office to make sure the correct amounts were listed for each account.

She was standing by Cory's desk when the sweet aroma of an expensive French perfume came drifting across the room.

Samantha lifted her head and saw the lithe

form of Denise Gerard, elegantly attired in a halter-necked pale blue chiffon dress. Her platinum-blond hair had been lifted away from her face and fell down the sun-tanned smoothness of her lovely bare back in a delicate cascade of elaborately styled curls.

In the brief moment when their eyes met, Samantha saw absolute shock freeze Denise's face. The perfectly formed mouth parted in surprise. "You! What have you—?" Before she had a chance to complete her sentence, Cory rose from his chair to welcome her. All thoughts of Samantha were forgotten as she floated toward him and placed a provocatively possessive kiss on his cheek.

"Darling, I was so anxious to see you that I couldn't stay away any longer. Did you miss me?" She flung her arms around his neck.

Cory looked over at Samantha. "That will be all, Miss Lorrimer. Why don't you see about straightening out the order forms with the back office?"

Samantha left the office, closing the door behind her. Denise Gerard's delicately soft laughter rang in her ears as she left the room and she felt a vise tighten around her heart. Denise Gerard had an air of feminine sophistication that Samantha knew she could never hope to attain. It was the air of complete assurance that came from growing up with wealth enormous enough to purchase anything one's heart desired. Her exquisite jewelry glistened on hands that had never been required to earn their own keep. They would soothe and caress the face of some adoring man, and, in return, he would give her his undying love. Samantha was sure that Cory Talbott was destined to be that man.

She was busy arranging the executed purchase slips into neat, orderly piles for delivery to the computer room when Cory and Denise came out of his office. Denise had linked her arm intimately through his and her openly possessive attitude made it quite evident that this was her man. Samantha remembered the arrogantly patronizing treatment she had suffered from Cory Talbott and knew that he would never subject the dainty Denise to such derisive abuse.

Cory freed his arm from Denise's, giving her smooth white hand a gentle pat. Then he walked to the desk and quickly scanned the tidy piles of order slips. "We've had a pretty full day, Miss Lorrimer. I'm going to be leaving now; why don't you go home and we can attend to these details in the morning?"

"It's quite all right, Mr. Talbott. I don't have school tonight so I can stay late and get this work cleared up for the computer room."

Cory frowned. "There's no rush on this work, and I don't like the idea of you staying late. These streets get pretty deserted once the stock market is closed."

Denise came up to Cory and gripped his arm, moving him impatiently toward the door. "Really, Cory, this isn't at all like you. You sound like an old mother hen. Miss Lorrimer can take care of herself. These career girls are quite independent, you know." She pulled Cory out the door while the perturbed frown was still covering his face.

Samantha worked rapidly, realizing that nervous energy was driving her on. It was eight o'clock and she had just finished entering the essential input data in the last client's chart when she heard heavy footsteps echo in the deserted hallway. She stiffened, suddenly remembering that she hadn't locked the outer door and was all alone in the desolate office.

She gripped the telephone receiver in her shaking hand and was halfway through dialing the police emergency number just as the door flew open. Cory Talbott's muscular frame blocked the open doorway and Samantha breathed a sigh of relief as she replaced the receiver. "You frightened me. I didn't expect you back this evening."

Cory's dark eyebrows knit together in anger. "You never listen, do you? I told you not to stay here after hours. Anyone could have walked through that door just as I did now. Then what would you have done?"

"I'm perfectly capable of handling the situation. I had already dialed the police emergency number when you walked in."

Cory snorted. "You could have been dead by the time they got here. I told you not to stay late and I expect my employees to listen when I tell them something. But I can see that you're determined to do everything in your power to exasperate me into losing my patience and firing you. Well, it won't work. I told you that you'd be sorry you ever dreamed up this wretched little scheme of yours and I meant it. You've probably spent your whole life twisting men around your beautiful little fingers, but I'm different. I find the new Samantha no more irresistible than I found the old Samantha, and I intend to keep you around just to prove it. You'll stay on at this job until I say you may leave, and I won't be angered into releasing you one minute before I want to. Now get your things together. We're leaving."

"I just want to take these to the computer room. I'll only be a minute." She picked up the pile of execution slips and Cory forcefully slammed her hand back on the desk.

"Drop them! I said we were leaving!" He grabbed her wrist and propelled her roughly toward the door.

Samantha glared at him as they rode down in the elevator. "It's no wonder you can't keep a secretary. You're an absolute tyrant!"

Cory looked at her coldly. "I don't believe there's anything dictatorial about an employer expecting an employee to obey his orders. I specifically told you not to work late and you deliberately disobeyed my wishes."

"I had work to complete. It was my job to see that those orders were ready for tomorrow morning's computer run."

Cory glared at her. "It is your job to obey my orders. Your only responsibility is to comply with my instructions."

"Well, I don't quite agree with you, Mr. Talbott. I have a responsibility to the company."

"I *am* the company, Miss Lorrimer. Your responsibility is to *me*." He led her to the car, slamming the door after she had seated herself. He settled himself behind the wheel and spoke in a carefully controlled voice. "Have you eaten?"

"I'm not hungry."

"I don't know why I even bother to ask you simple questions. Well, I don't imagine you have, and you're so angry that you'll probably go to bed without any dinner, so we'll have something to eat before I take you home."

Samantha turned toward Cory; icicles dripped from her voice. "I said I wasn't hungry."

Cory snorted. "Well I am. So you can watch me eat if you have no appetite."

"Didn't you eat with Miss Gerard?"

"I wasn't hungry at the time and Miss Gerard developed a sudden headache, so I took her home."

"Oh," Samantha said. "So you came seeking me out as her replacement."

Cory's eyes glinted mischievously, as if he were relaxing and coming out of his black mood. "My dear Miss Lorrimer, you could never replace Denise. There's absolutely no comparison."

Samantha bristled with anger. "Oh, you make me so mad!"

Cory kept driving. His face was now totally relaxed. "Yes, I do, don't I?" He flashed a wicked smile in her direction.

The car headed uptown, moving past the twin towers of the World Trade Center. Samantha watched in wonder as the stark office buildings of lower Manhattan gave way to the extravagant opulence of midtown, where large, impressive department stores mingled with elegant little boutiques and restaurants.

But this world was hardly available to a girl living on a secretarial salary, and Samantha wistfully turned away from the tempting store windows. "Where are we going? I'm really tired and I want to get home."

"Don't worry. You'll get home in good time."

He circled the block and stopped the car in front of the red-canopied entrance of an elegant Fifth Avenue hotel. A doorman hastened to open the door for Samantha while a parking attendant took the car keys from Cory. Then Cory placed his hand on Samantha's waist and guided her firmly through the brightly polished brass door. They took the elevator to the rooftop restaurant, where the softly haunting tones of a romantic melody drifted through the open arch of a candlelit café.

The headwaiter greeted Cory by name and led them to a secluded table for two overlooking Central Park. Cory ordered a martini for himself and a chilled glass of white wine for Samantha. Then, without asking what she wanted to eat, he told the waiter to bring the usual and settled back in his seat. His eyes were inquisitive but strangely relaxed as they studied Samantha.

"I like to come here because I get a slightly different view of Central Park than I do from my terrace. You remember that view, don't you?"

Samantha colored, remembering the occasion only too well. She took a long sip of her wine and turned her face toward the wall of glass at her side. Cory might be discussing the view from the window, but his eyes were riveted on her profile, and she nervously bit at her lower lip, trying to control the tension that was building within her.

"I asked if you remembered the view from my apartment. Are you going to answer me or do you intend to sulk all evening?"

"I'm not sulking. I don't like being here. I'm tired and I want to go home."

"Then you should have gone home at the proper time. Just consider this dinner as part of your job, and if you find it a tedious chore, I suggest you obey my instructions in the future. Unlike you, Miss Lorrimer, I mean what I say. I don't play games with no thought of the possible consequences."

"I'm sorry for what I did. I've apologized. What more do you want? I don't see any reason for you to get so angry over it."

Cory narrowed his eyes at Samantha. "I don't get angry, Miss Lorrimer; I get even. Right now I'm exacting payment for the fun you had at my expense."

"I didn't have any fun! I only wanted a responsible job where I could learn about the financial industry."

Cory finished his drink before answering her. "Well, I daresay you have achieved your goal. You must admit, you *are* learning about the investment industry, aren't you?"

Samantha shook her head. "Yes, the job is fine. I really enjoy my work. It's just . . ."

"Just what, Miss Lorrimer?"

"Oh, I don't know. I guess it's nothing," Samantha said. There was no way she could tell him that he was the one who was making things difficult for her. If he would just leave her alone, perhaps she could gain control of herself, but she would never survive if he kept pressuring her the way he seemed determined to do.

Dinner arrived and Samantha thoroughly enjoyed the succulent rack of lamb with small roasted potatoes. After dinner, Cory insisted she try the restaurant's specialty, rich black coffee laced with a chocolaty liqueur and topped with a dollop of whipped cream. She leaned back in her seat, savoring the soothing warmth of the sweetly intoxicating liquid.

Cory watched as she finished her drink. He leaned forward, put out his index finger, drew it across her upper lip, and came away with a trace of whipped cream. His finger moved slowly between her lips until she opened them and licked away the cream with the tip of her tongue.

Her breath caught in her throat and she moved back, frightened by the wild sensations that were coursing through her body.

Cory dropped his hand, but continued studying her face. Without shifting his gaze, he came around to the back of her chair and placed his hands on her shoulders. "Let's dance."

"I'd really rather not." Samantha's voice was a tight little squeak. "I have a lot of work to do tomorrow and I want to be in early."

Cory took her hand and lifted her from the chair. "There's no need to be in early when you've spent the night with the boss." He looked into her eyes and gently placed his finger over her lips, effectively stifling any reply she might have made to his suggestive statement.

The band was playing a leisurely romantic melody, and Cory, still holding Samantha's hand, deftly turned her into the warm circle of his waiting arms. He brought the hand he was holding up to his cheek and his other arm moved swiftly to Samantha's waist, molding her unguarded body to the hard masculine strength of his own. Samantha's other hand was trapped against his jacket, providing the only barrier between the tender softness of her rapidly rising breasts and the iron wall of his own muscular chest. She tried to put some distance between them, but Cory took her hand from his cheek and placed it behind his neck. Then he used his newly freed hand to stroke her hair, slowly removing the confining pins, releasing it from its bun and gently forcing her face down against the swiftly beating tattoo of his heart.

His hands began moving in unison, caressing her body with the arousing touch of an experienced lover as his mouth came down to nuzzle her earlobe and kiss the softly pulsing cord in her neck. Samantha's veins began throbbing with intoxicating heat. They were so close that she was sure he could feel the rapid beat of her heart.

Cory's breath was warm and soft as he whispered in her ear. "Relax, it's only a dance." He circled his left hand to her waist and began sensuously massaging her against his strong, masculine contours. "Come on, unbend. You feel as stiff as a board."

Samantha pressed her hand against his chest and drew her head back to look into his face. Instantly, she realized her mistake. His mouth swooped down and covered hers with a gentle butterfly touch which hardened as his hand rose to support her head and press her lips more firmly to his.

She twisted her head and looked up at him; her barely audible voice was a husky whisper while her limpid eyes pleaded with him. "Please let me go."

Cory's features tensed, but he loosened his arms and gently rested his hand on her waist while he guided her back to the table. She picked up her handbag and, without uttering a word, they left the building and retrieved the car.

Cory moved into the stream of traffic and, after a few minutes, turned to her. He seemed completely unaffected by the dance which had so totally unnerved Samantha. "I don't suppose you'd consider staying at my place and saving me the trip downtown? Then I could take you into work in the morning and no one would dare criticize you for being late."

Samantha's tension turned into unbridled anger. "No, of course they wouldn't. They would be too busy gossiping about us. My reputation wouldn't be worth very much when the office grapevine finished with me. Why don't you go find your precious Denise? I'm sure she could keep you happy tonight!"

"Indeed she could. Unlike you, she's affection-ate and soft and doesn't have a nasty tongue." He pulled the car to a halt, and Samantha realized that they were in front of her building. She reached for the door but Cory caught her hand.

"A lady always waits for a gentleman to open the car door for her."

She sat back in her seat while Cory got out of the car and came up beside her door.

"I wasn't aware of any gentlemen in the immediate vicinity."

"Cute, but you'll have to pay for that." He opened the car door and waited while Samantha walked toward the house.

She motioned him away impatiently.

Cory didn't seem to notice and he held the outer door open for her in such a way that she had to walk under his arm in order to enter the lobby. Samantha walked on ahead, aware that he was still following her, his firm footsteps echoing in the empty hall.

She stopped at her apartment door and took her key out of her purse. Immediately, Cory's large hand covered hers and gently took the key. He unlocked the door and returned the key to Samantha. She took it without looking and moved to enter the apartment. Then he reached out, grasping her shoulders, and swung her back toward him. "The evening isn't over—yet."

The fire burning in his eyes was a searing combination of anger and desire. Savagely, he pulled her toward him, bringing his mouth down to meet hers. There was no tenderness in his kiss. He asked her for nothing; he was demanding—crushing her body to his with his strong arms—bruising her lips with the powerful force of his own.

Samantha felt the blood in her veins turn molten and she was helplessly caught in a whirlwind of passion as her arms rose to encircle his neck and her lips moved in fervent response to his. She felt herself transported to an unknown region where she cared about nothing except Cory's touch on her welcoming flesh, and she willingly bent her body in reply to his masculine demands.

When he felt the hunger in her response, his touch softened. The steel hands that imprisoned her became tantalizing feathers, stroking her body, teasing her emotions. His lips moved to the curve of her jaw, edging ever downward; she arched her neck, exposing her tingling flesh to the searing blaze of his mouth.

Her fingers traveled to his chest, twirling around the buttons—opening them—slipping inside to touch the warmth of his flesh. She could feel the rapid beat of his heart pounding against her caressing hand. The sensation sent sharp quivers of delight racing through her body and she turned her face toward his, hoping that for once she had breached the bonds of his inflexible control.

She had no chance to see anything; as soon as she turned her face toward him his lips recaptured hers, seductively urging her to increasingly dangerous heights of passion. She clung to him desperately, wanting to get even closer, to know every inch of him. She could deny him nothing; her entire being yearned for him—

begged him to take her deeper into the labyrinth of love.

Then, suddenly, she felt Cory's arms rise to his neck and he gently released himself from her embrace. He looked down at her quivering lips, still soft from the savagely demanding assault of his own, and a mocking glint came into his eyes.

"I'll consider that kiss partial payment for your verbal abuse of a few minutes ago." He placed his hand on the doorknob and opened the door, letting a confused and hurt Samantha walk into the apartment. "Lock the door behind you. There's no telling what sort of ungentlemanly creature might be lurking in the darkness." His arrogant laughter echoed in Samantha's ears long after his footsteps had faded.

She walked into the bedroom and began getting ready for bed. Snuggling under the covers, she stared at the ceiling, remembering the tingling sensation of Cory's lips on hers and the fires that his caressing hands had kindled in the depths of her body. There wasn't one inch of her flesh that hadn't responded to him and wanted him to continue.

The last thing in the world she had wanted was to fall in love with Cory Talbott, but she had, and she knew that it would take every ounce of her willpower to resist his advances if he ever really decided that he wanted her.

Cory spent the following day at the corporate headquarters of a large company, attending a directors' meeting. Samantha breathed a sigh of relief as she turned to her work, liberated from the tension that Cory's presence always evoked in her.

The weekend provided her with an additional respite from the torment of Cory's presence. Janet was now spending most of her free time with Jim, so Samantha virtually had the apartment to herself. She heard Janet leave early Sunday morning to accompany Jim to a producer's house, then rolled over and went back to sleep.

An insistent ringing played a cacophonous melody in her ear, and she reached out to silence the alarm clock but discovered that it was already off. Frowning, she cast a sleepy eye at the bedside phone. But the harsh ring was from the doorbell, she realized as she came awake. Snatching her robe from the foot of the bed, she pulled it on and, without bothering to fasten the belt, padded barefoot toward the door.

She was still groggy with sleep as she called out, "Who is it?"

"It's me; Cory."

Samantha's sleepy mind tried to sort out the situation. She was quite sure it was Sunday. She wasn't expected at work. So why was Cory Talbott here? Had something happened? Was he hurt, and turning to her for help?

She opened the door quickly. Cory walked in and she pressed her hands into his chest. "What happened? What's wrong?"

Cory's eyes swept Samantha's lightly clothed body and came to rest on her face. He shut the door and folded her into his arms. Holding her tenderly against him he lowered his lips and caressed the crown of her hair. "Nothing's wrong, Samantha. What are you so worried about?"

Samantha sighed with relief. Then she remembered her disheveled appearance. Her robe was completely open at the front, exposing her short nylon pajamas, which were entirely too flimsy and sheer. The lightweight fabric rested loosely against her body, clinging sensuously to every feminine curve and highlighting the very features it sought to cover. Her long shapely legs were totally bare, and she could feel the nervous bumps rising on her skin as Cory's eyes devoured her.

"Then why are you here?" she said, standing and pulling the robe snugly around her waist while she tied the belt in a secure double knot.

The fire in Cory's eyes was banked as he relaxed into the rocking chair by the window. "I was in the neighborhood and took a chance that you might be home."

"Well, I am home. Now what do you want?"

"My, my, not at all friendly this morning, are you?"

"I don't have to be friendly. Today is Sunday, and Talbott Associates doesn't pay for my services on the weekend."

Cory smiled indulgently. "A good thing, too. It looks as if you intend to spend the day in bed, and, as you know, Talbott Associates doesn't provide its clients with that sort of service."

Samantha did her best both to ignore his taunting and to keep her anger in check. "Would you please just tell me what you want and then leave? I don't need to be subjected to your insults on the weekend."

Cory's face became suddenly serious. He left the rocker and came to sit on the couch beside Samantha. "I haven't said anything to insult you, Samantha. Can't you tell when a man is teasing? Actually, I've come to apologize for my behavior the other evening. I did promise that I wouldn't make any advances to you and I certainly broke my word on that occasion. I want to assure you that it won't ever happen again. In fact, I'm going to spend the entire day with you just to prove how proper my behavior will be from now on."

Samantha shook her head. It was amazing, how their relationship seemed to change with each twist in the conversation. "All right, I accept your apology, but it wasn't necessary to come all the way down here to tell me. You could have phoned."

"And then you would have thought up some excuse for not spending the day with me, wouldn't you?"

"I don't have to think of an excuse. I can't spend the day with you. I have too many things to do."

"Such as what?"

"I . . . I . . . I have to do some homework and I like to read the Sunday paper and I have some letters to write."

"All of which can wait for another occasion. What you really mean is that you don't want to spend the day with me, and that's not fair because I deserve an opportunity to show you that I can be completely trusted."

Samantha began to waver. Despite what he thought, the problem was actually that she wanted to spend the day with him too much.

He saw her hesitate and, taking her hands in his, lifted her from the sofa. "Get dressed. And don't take too long; I haven't had any breakfast and I'm hungry." He led Samantha to the bedroom and closed the door behind her, then called through, "I have a surprise for you, too."

Samantha washed quickly, then walked to the closet, trying to decide what to wear.

"Wear something casual." Cory's voice echoed through the closed door as if he could read her thoughts.

Cory's appreciative eyes told Samantha how well her outfit looked when she reentered the living room a few minutes later. The muted beige of her linen pants matched the broad stripes in the cowl-necked cotton knit shirt which clung lightly to her feminine curves as it fell loosely to her hips. He waited while she got her handbag, then escorted her to the street and walked right past his car. She looked at him quizzically, but he took her hand and kept walking.

"I'm not taking the car. We're not going very far; besides, walking will help you work up an appetite."

Samantha laughed. "If I work up much more of an appetite there won't be enough food in the entire city to satisfy me. I'm starving. It's past noon and I haven't had my breakfast yet."

"I promise this will be worth waiting for. It will be the best breakfast you've ever had."

As they walked, the sidewalks became extremely crowded and the people overflowed into the streets. The melodious lyrics of an old Italian love song came drifting through the lazy September air, and Samantha raised her head inquisitively. Cory smiled intriguingly and led her on. The entire crowd seemed to be going in one direction, and Samantha and Cory just followed along. They turned the corner and the music grew progressively louder. Multicolored lights hung from the trees and buildings, as if it were Christmas. The street was closed to traffic, and small food-vending carts lined the sidewalks, filling the summer air with their tantalizing aromas.

"The Festival of San Gennaro," Cory said. "The parishioners of the local church celebrate it annually. People come from all over to see each other and enjoy the homemade delicacies. I make it a point never to miss it, and this year I'm delighted to share it with you." He led her to a small cart and purchased some crusty bread, sausages and cheese. He handed some to Samantha and they strolled through the streets, munching on their unorthodox breakfast, the first of the many Italian delicacies Samantha was to sample that day. They joined the festive crowds dancing the tarantella and singing plaintive arias from Italian operas. Finally Cory took her elbow and led her away from the throng of people.

"It's getting late; I think we'd better be going."

The streets grew quieter as they walked toward Samantha's building. She had never enjoyed herself so much. True to his word, Cory had been a perfect gentleman. Not once had he teased her or tried to get her angry. His arm rested easily on her waist while they silently covered the distance to her apartment. All too soon they were at the door. Cory took her key and unlocked it, then guided her in.

He remained by the open door, barely crossing over the threshold. "Switch on the lights and check the apartment; I'll wait here."

Samantha did as he said and quickly returned. "Everything is fine. There's really no need to be so cautious."

"Maybe not," Cory said, "but I think you take too many chances. This is New York City, not some small farming town."

"I'm used to taking care of myself. Don't worry, Cory." His name still felt funny on her tongue, but he had insisted that she use it, at least outside the office.

"So I gather. Perhaps you're too used to taking care of yourself. Sometimes a person can be too independent." His voice grew low and husky. "There's nothing wrong with letting someone who cares for you take care of you."

Samantha looked into Cory's eyes. There was a tenderness and concern she had never seen there before.

He looked closely into her face as desire flickered then faded under the careful control exhibited in his cool gray eyes. She held her breath and met his gaze, hoping his eyes would read the message of love hers were sending. But he just inhaled deeply and turned to walk quickly down the stairway.

Samantha closed the door, feeling cold and lonely, despite the warmth of the mid-September evening.

Chapter Seven

The hostility on Mrs. Harrison's face was apparent as her words cut into Samantha. "You must be very proud of yourself. It's all over the office about how you pulled the wool over my eyes. Well, if there's one thing Mr. Talbott and I cannot abide, it's dishonesty. I'm surprised he hasn't dismissed you by now."

Samantha had been expecting a scene when Mrs. Harrison returned, so she was at least partially prepared for this assault. "I haven't been dismissed because Mr. Talbott realizes I'm a good secretary, and that's all that really matters, isn't it? Why should my physical appearance make any difference one way or the other?"

Mrs. Harrison eyed Samantha distastefully. "But it does make a difference, doesn't it? Perhaps you think that by using alluring makeup and wearing seductive clothing you'll be able to worm your way into Mr. Talbott's affections. But it won't work, you know. Cory Talbott won't be taken in by your little scheme."

"Can't anyone understand that all I ever wanted was the opportunity to do a good job? I'm not interested in stealing Cory Talbott from Denise Gerard; there's no possible way he could ever prefer me to her. Now will you please leave me alone? I have some very important work to get out for Mr. Talbott!"

Mrs. Harrison turned on her heel and left the office. Samantha sighed and went back to her work, but she felt sure she had not heard the last from Mrs. Harrison.

Samantha was pondering this unpleasant state of affairs when the telephone rang. She answered it and was surprised to hear Denise Gerard.

"I'm sorry, Miss Gerard, but Mr. Talbott hasn't come in yet."

"That's quite all right, Miss Lorrimer," Denise said. "I wanted to speak with you, privately, before Cory got into the office. I noticed the unusual change in your appearance the other week, and I've since heard more about the situation from Mrs. Harrison. I just wanted you to know that Cory and I are practically engaged, so don't think you can use your feminine wiles to generate his interest in you."

Samantha gripped the telephone receiver in an effort to control her anger. "I'm sorry my appearance is so disturbing to everyone, but I don't care to discuss the situation since I have no romantic interest in Mr. Talbott. My dealings with him are strictly of a business nature." And don't I wish they weren't, she thought to herself.

"I'm glad to hear that," Denise said. "I'd hate to see you get hurt. Well, I'm so glad we've had this little chat. And, Miss Lorrimer, there's no need to mention our discussion to Cory. Let's just keep it between us girls." Then she severed the connection.

Samantha stood staring at the lifeless telephone receiver, then slammed it down on the hook. Imagine Denise talking to her like that. It was bad enough that she had to put up with Mrs. Harrison's tirades and Cory's heartless overtures. There was no reason why she had to be insulted by Denise, too. She sighed deeply, finding it increasingly difficult to concentrate on her work when all these emotional problems clouded the situation.

Cory came in at ten o'clock and glanced at the papers on Samantha's desk before speaking. "Are there any messages for me?" he said as he walked into his private office.

Samantha followed him, carrying a stack of pink message slips with her. Cory leaned back in his chair, quickly considering each message. Then he told Samantha to place a call to Los Angeles and bring him his coffee. Samantha did as she was told, amazed that Cory could put the events of the weekend behind him so easily.

When Billy came in with the morning mail, he stopped to chat for a few minutes. They were talking quietly when Mrs. Harrison opened the door and looked at them coldly, as if she were observing some lewd act.

"Don't you two have anything better to do than sit around chattering with each other? I certainly intend to speak to Mr. Talbott about this, Samantha. You know quite well how I feel about your little deception, and if you can't even be bothered to do your job . . ." She walked past Samantha's desk and knocked lightly on Cory's door.

Samantha rose quickly. "You can't do that. Mr. Talbott is on the telephone. I can't permit you to barge in on him like that."

Mrs. Harrison placed her hand on the doorknob and looked disdainfully at Samantha. "I'll take full responsibility for my actions, Miss Lorrimer." She opened the door and entered Cory's office.

Cory looked up at them with undisguised annoyance. He raised his hand and motioned Mrs. Harrison into the room, waving Samantha away. Mrs. Harrison smiled sweetly as Samantha returned to her desk. In a short while the phone light went out, indicating that Cory had terminated his conversation. Then the intercom buzzed and he told her to hold all calls until he had completed his buisness with Mrs. Harrison.

It was at least an hour later when Mrs. Harrison left the room, the icy stare she directed at Samantha an indication of her mood. Samantha was contemplating the situation when Cory buzzed her on the intercom.

"Please bring me a fresh cup of coffee."

Samantha got the coffee, placed it silently on

Cory's desk, and turned to leave the room. Cory's booming voice called her back.

"Sit down; there's something I'd like to discuss with you."

Samantha edged herself into the chair at the side of the desk. She wondered if Mrs. Harrison had convinced him to fire her and end his vengeful game. Much as she hated the situation she was in, she couldn't face the thought of never seeing Cory again. Her mind might push him away, but her flesh kept reaching out and willing him closer. The nerve ends in the pit of her stomach tightened into jumpy little knots and her fingers were balled so tightly that she could feel her nails biting into the palms of her hands.

He tilted his chair back and placed the tips of his fingers together, tapping them lightly as he gazed thoughtfully at the ceiling. Then, in one swift jolting movement, he lowered his chair and dropped his hands to the desk. "Mrs. Harrison isn't too pleased with your work. She seems to think that you've been wasting company time to further some sort of private relationship with Billy Haskins."

Samantha forgot her nervousness in her anger at Cory's remark. "That's absolutely ridiculous. Billy and I are just friends."

Cory's face remained impassive. "Nevertheless, you must admit that you do spend quite a bit of time in his company. Mrs. Harrison said she broke up an intimate conversation when she came to see me just now."

Samantha's eyes flashed with anger. "We

were talking. So what? Why don't you ask Mrs. Harrison what's really bothering her? She's mad because I don't look like an ugly old spinster anymore; it has nothing to do with Billy. She wants me fired!"

Cory's eyes flashed arrogantly. "Miss Lorrimer, you seem to forget that neither you nor Mrs. Harrison makes the final decisions regarding who is employed by this firm. However, I don't like this kind of discord within the company. So try to make your peace with Mrs. Harrison and avoid any personal conversations with Billy in the future."

Samantha definitely felt that she was being unfairly chastised. Her involvement with Billy was so casual that she couldn't understand why Cory was making so much of it, unless, of course, he wanted to make sure that she had absolutely no friends in the office.

It seemed as if Cory were tightening the prison he had built around her. She was beginning to wonder if a career was worth all these problems. But then she remembered that if you wanted something badly enough you had to be prepared to fight for it, and she wanted a career in the financial field as much as she had ever wanted anything—except for Cory's love. There was no doubt in her mind that in spite of everything he could teach her a lot about the investment industry, and right now she seemed destined to spend her life as a career woman.

"I'll try to be more friendly to Mrs. Harrison, but I doubt it will do much good. She wants to believe the worst about me. As for Billy, I'll confine my conversations with him to after business hours."

Cory nodded complacently. "I'm glad we understand each other. Go back to whatever you were doing."

Cory's eyes burned into Samantha's back as she left his office. The morning's events had made it almost impossible for her to concentrate on her work and she was completing some neglected filing when James Carson walked in. He tilted his head and studied her as she turned to greet him.

"Well, I must say, the scenery around here is certainly improving." He winked at Samantha. "Is Cory free for lunch?" He perched on the edge of Samantha's desk, waiting while she buzzed Cory on the intercom.

Cory opened his door almost immediately. "How are you, Jim? Shouldn't you be in rehearsals? I understand the show is opening in Boston next month."

"That's true, and there are still a few bugs we have to iron out. I hope we can take care of them before incurring the wrath of the New York critics. Actually, rehearsals start at two o'clock this afternoon and I wanted to get my affairs in order before I really become involved with the show. It may be difficult to reach me once things get moving, and I don't want to leave any loose ends hanging around."

Cory motioned Jim into his office and instructed Samantha to hold all his calls until they had concluded their conference. He closed the door, and Samantha resumed her filing. She had just filed the last piece of correspondence when Janet walked into the office.

Samantha's voice reflected her surprise. "Janet, what are you doing here?"

Janet smiled nonchalantly. "Jim asked me to meet him here. He promised to take me to lunch before rehearsal."

"Are you sure? I think he's going to lunch with Cory. Anyway, have a seat; he ought to be out soon."

She was about to ask Janet about the play when Jim came strolling out of Cory's office. His face lit up as he walked over to Janet and placed a kiss lightly on her cheek. "How do you manage to look lovelier each time I see you? You'd think I'd be used to beautiful women after all my years in Hollywood, but I don't think I've ever run across anyone as exquisite as you are."

Janet smiled. "I can't tell you how happy that makes me, because I feel exactly the same way about you. But I'm afraid Sam doesn't approve. In fact, she keeps warning me about your terrible reputation."

Jim shook his head. "I can see that if I'm going to conquer Janet's heart I have to conquer you first. So I'll begin my campaign by taking you to lunch today."

"I'm sorry, Jim. I'd love to, but I can't. I've got a ton of work to finish." She saw Jim's eyes drift behind her and turned to see Cory standing in the doorway.

Jim put one arm around Janet's bare shoulders as he stared lazily at Cory. "Since when are you running a slave ship here? Don't you even give the hired help time off for lunch anymore?"

Cory eyed Samantha disdainfully. "Why do you ask? Has Samantha been grumbling? I told her there would be times when we'd have to have our lunches at our desks. This is a demanding business and she knows it. If she has any problems I'd certainly rather have her come to me with them instead of discussing them with a client." His remarks were addressed to Jim but he looked meaningfully at Samantha.

Jim was totally unmoved by Cory's remarks. "On the contrary, Samantha never uttered one word of complaint. The opinions expressed were entirely those of Jim Carson and no one else. I was merely trying to shame you into allowing Samantha to join us for lunch today."

Cory's mouth quirked derisively. "There's no reason why she can't have lunch with you today. We had a busy day yesterday, but the backlog has been cleared away and now it's all in the hands of the computer room."

"Then it's settled," Jim said. "I'm treating everyone to lunch, and we'd better get started or Janet and I will be late for our rehearsal."

Uncomfortably, Samantha joined the others as they left the building. Jim hailed a cab and gave the driver the name of a famous German restaurant in lower Manhattan. The restaurant was a New York landmark, established in the latter part of the last century, and its decor reflected the conservative masculine aura of that era. Dark oak paneled the walls and rich red carpeting covered the floor of a room that was softly illuminated by hushed amber lights. The entire atmosphere gave one the impression of dining in the book-lined library of a nineteenth-century country squire.

Jim and Cory were both well-known there. They were shown into a private room where their waiter catered to their desires solicitously. The meal started with a tasty goose liver pâté; then, as a main course, Jim ordered Rhine wine and schnitzel. Samantha had always believed that German food was heavy and tasteless, but this veal was light and delectably prepared. She was thoroughly satisfied when the meal ended with a delicious torte and rich black coffee.

When they left the restaurant, Jim explained that he and Janet would have to leave for rehearsals immediately, leaving Cory and Samantha to return to the office. They watched as Jim waved good-bye from a cab, then Cory turned to Samantha.

"It's such a beautiful day and that was a filling lunch. How would you feel about walking back to the office?"

Samantha smiled. "I'm used to walking. I'm a country girl, remember? But aren't you in a rush to get back? It's nearly two o'clock and walking will take at least half an hour."

"Samantha, I told you, we have no set hours and no one will question your taking time off as long as you're with me." His hand came up to casually encircle her waist as if it were the most natural thing in the world for him to be doing.

"I'm glad to see that you're wearing sensible walking shoes, now you won't have any trouble keeping up with me." His arm tightened around Samantha's waist and drew her closer to him as he continued strolling at a leisurely pace.

Samantha felt the nerve ends in her body tense as his arm circled her waist so possessively. He was so casual and yet so deliberate in his relationship with her. Either he saw her as a colorless fixture in his office or as the perpetrator of some horrible scheme to deceive him. At no time did he visualize her simply as an attractive woman. Indeed, he had told her that she could in no way compare with Denise, who was his idea of what a desirable woman should be. Yet, for whatever reason, Cory was deliberately teasing her and trying to arouse her.

They strolled through Washington Square Park and Cory led Samantha to a grassy area where a folk singer was filling the air with the lilting poetry of his plaintive guitar. They paused to listen, then Cory lowered himself to the grass and pulled her down next to him, cradling her head against his shoulder.

Samantha's heart began to beat wildly, but the soft monotone of the folk singer's quiet voice combined with the wine she had consumed at lunch to lull the warning bells that were chiming in her brain, and she made no effort to resist when Cory lay back, pulling her head onto his chest. Sighing contentedly, she settled herself deeper into the pillow of his racing heart as his questing hand gently caressed the soft skin of her upper arm, pulling her closer with every tender stroke.

Samantha's defenses were completely gone,

and she no longer cared about Cory's intentions
or his love for Denise Gerard. All she cared about
was the warm glow of contentment that was
spreading through her body as she lay securely
within the crook of his strong, comforting arm.
She knew that she would be satisfied to remain
like this forever. The fall day was unusually
warm and the wine had made her drowsy, and
soon Samantha had relaxed into sleep.

A sudden movement made her stir uneasily.
She snuggled deeper into the warmth beneath
her, unwilling to relinquish the languid comfort
that was flowing through her veins. She moaned
with annoyance as she felt herself being lifted
and her position shifted.

The soft cushion her cheek had been resting
on was gone and she was on her back, supported
only by a large muscular hand that was combing
through her hair, releasing it from its pins and
slowly fanning it out with gently caressing
strokes.

Tender lips came down to plant a soft kiss on
her shuttered eyelids and they fluttered open to
stare through sleep-laden lashes at the expressionless face of Cory Talbott. Samantha felt
herself hazily wondering what Cory was doing,
but she was too relaxed from her unexpected
nap to make any sudden movements and she lay
motionless beneath him as his face came down
to meet her lips in a softly questing kiss.

Her yielding lips answered his kiss as he
suddenly became more demanding, hardening
his lips against hers until he had forced them to
follow the probing motions of his own. One hand

made circular motions through her loosened hair as the other left her arm and began loosening the top button of her blouse, his exploring fingers traveling beneath it to gently tease the upper swell of one firm breast.

That burning touch set off an alarm in Samantha's head. Immediately, she tensed, and her body became rigid beneath Cory's as she pushed her arms against his chest and twisted away from him. He released her quickly and sat up, running his fingers through his hair while his eyes studied her as she hurriedly buttoned her blouse with nervously fumbling fingers. She rose to her feet abruptly; then she smoothed her skirt, brushing away the blades of grass that were clinging to it.

A hazy gray twilight was descending on the park and she glanced anxiously at her watch. "It's five-thirty! We must have fallen asleep." She bit her lip nervously. "I'm sorry . . . Cory. Sleep can make people do funny things. I hope you won't hold this against me. I know you don't believe me, but I really don't want to do anything to jeopardize my job."

Cory's voice assumed the frigid tones of the ruthless money manager. "No, Samantha, I won't do anything to interfere with your career. That's all you really want in life, isn't it?" He grasped Samantha's hand angrily. "There's no need for you to return to work today. I'll walk you to your house and take a cab back to the office so I can pick up my car."

Samantha shook her head. "I'm not going home. I have school tonight and I'm right near the university, so I'll walk right on to class. I can share a book with someone. I'll be perfectly all right on my own."

Cory shook his head. "O.K., if that's what you want. What time does your class end?"

Samantha considered for a moment. "About nine-thirty. Why?"

Cory's eyes studied her face. "No reason. See you later, Samantha." Without another word, he turned and walked away.

Night school always revitalized Samantha, and she was engaged in a lively conversation with several other members of her class when she heard a familiar voice call her as she walked beneath the arch of Washington Square. She turned an astonished face in Cory Talbott's direction. "Cory, what are you doing here?"

The other students waved good-bye and walked on as Cory came up and placed his arm casually around her shoulders. "I had some buisness to attend to at the office and it kept me longer than I expected, so I thought I might as well drive you home since I was still in the area."

He opened the car door, waited while she seated herself, then settled himself behind the wheel. "Besides, I wanted to apologize for this afternoon. I wouldn't want it to interfere with our ability to work together."

Samantha sighed. "Don't be silly. It meant nothing to me; you can consider it forgotten already."

Cory smiled. "I'm glad you feel that way, Samantha. It's refreshing to hear such a reasonable response from a woman. I was afraid I might have frightened you, or even awakened some romantic desires on your part, but I did neither of those things, did I?" He looked at her expectantly.

Samantha turned her head away so he couldn't see her trembling lower lip. "No, of course not. I told you what my feelings were."

Cory sighed in exasperation and shook his head.

The trip to Samantha's house was accomplished in complete silence, and Cory left her at the door, saying, "I'll see you tomorrow morning" and walked quickly back to the car.

She leaned against her door, listening to his angry footsteps. He thought she was just like him, completely heartless. He could never picture her as a woman who was as warm and loving as Denise Gerard. She blushed with shame as she realized what might have happened if she hadn't managed a quick recovery of her senses in the park. Cory's revenge would have been complete beyond his wildest dreams if she had succumbed to his touch, only to be thrown away after he had achieved his goal and returned to the warm and loving arms of Denise, all the while laughing at the victory he had achieved over Samantha.

Chapter Eight

The next morning Samantha found the office crowded with people she didn't recognize. The building security guards were clearing the area, and when she asked what the problem was, one handed her the latest copy of a well-known women's magazine.

Samantha entered her office and leaned gratefully against the closed door, happy to be away from the chaos outside. Then she settled herself at her desk and looked at the cover of the magazine. There, along with those of several other men, was Cory Talbott's picture. The headline read: *The World's Ten Most Eligible Bachelors*. Samantha opened the magazine to the page where the article began and flipped quickly to the paragraphs about Cory. It gave his age as thirty-five, described him as a self-made millionaire, fond of auto racing and tennis, then listed the name of his firm and even his address before going on to talk in more detail about the man and what made him so attractive to women.

Samantha was engrossed in the article when the telephone rang. She picked up the receiver and her ears were assaulted by the unbridled anger in Cory's voice.

"Have you seen that blasted magazine article?"

"Yes," Samantha said. "I'm reading it right now. You've become quite the celebrity, haven't you?"

She could hear Cory snarling viciously at the other end of the line. "Cut it out, will you, Samantha! I fail to see any humor in the situation. My apartment is under seige from snoopy reporters wanting additional information and aggressive women claiming to be just what every lonely bachelor needs. How are things down at the office?"

"There was a mob scene when I arrived, but the security guards have started to clear the halls, so I imagine most of the crowd is out on the street by now."

"Blast," Cory said. "I've got too much work to start dealing with a horde of nosy reporters and neurotic women. Listen carefully, Samantha. I want you to go home and pack whatever you'll need. We're going away for a few days."

Samantha hesitated. "Going away? I don't understand."

Cory sounded exasperated. "Come on, Samantha. I've dealt with enough confused women this morning to last me a lifetime. So please, spare me the hysterics. I'm not suggesting an amorous tryst. I have work that has to get done and it's quite obvious that we can't work in the city. I have a beach house on Long Island and I hope we can find some privacy there. Very few peple know about it. Thank heaven it wasn't mentioned in that blasted article."

"I can't go away with you, Cory. It just wouldn't look right. What would people think?"

"You know, Samantha, this situation is really unbelievable. There are hordes of women waiting outside my door, pleading for the chance to be alone with me, and I happen to need the services of my secretary, who acts as if she'd rather spend her day with Attila the Hun. Look, Samantha, you should know by now that if something is going to happen, it can happen in a crowded city park. I assure you I'm not going to force my attentions on you. I merely want to keep my firm operating until this tempest blows over, and in order to do that I need your services and a quiet place in which to work. Believe me, your body is nothing new to me. I'm sure I'll be able to keep my hands off you—unless, of course, your scheming little mind is really hoping for just the opposite?"

Samantha fumed, but she refused to rise to his taunt. The less he knew about her feelings and intentions the better. Whatever he might think of her, she knew that any relationship into which he might lead her would not be as easily shrugged off by her as it would be by him, and she was not going to walk willingly into that kind of pain.

"I'm sorry, Cory, but there's no way I can see myself being alone with you for several days in some little beach cottage. Why don't you take Mrs. Harrison?"

"Mrs. Harrison has to stay behind to run the office. Besides, I never said we would be alone. That's just something you conjured up. My housekeeper and butler will be joining us. So everything will be perfectly proper. Although I must say, you're pretty narrow-minded for a liberated woman."

Samantha was glad that Cory couldn't see her face as an embarrassed blush began to creep across it. She sounded chastened, even to herself, as she reluctantly faced the fact that she had no valid excuse for refusing him and told him she would go.

Samantha could hear Cory's deep rich chuckle coming through the phone line. "Samantha, you never cease to amaze me. Go home and pack your bags; I'll be by to pick you up in an hour. Try to be outside. I don't want to waste any more time than is absolutely necessary."

A little over an hour later she found herself sitting next to Cory as he drove carefully through the crowded city, eventually moving onto the Long Island Expressway and heading away from the city.

"You look as if you're a million miles away.

What could possibly be making you so sad?" Cory asked, breaking the uncomfortable silence that had filled the car since he had picked her up.

"I was just thinking about the farm. I wonder if anyone should ever leave such a beautiful place and move to a crowded city like this."

Cory shrugged. "You said you wanted a career in the financial industry and there's no way you could ever achieve any real success without working on Wall Street. That's where the action is and that's where you have to be if you want to make it."

Samantha nodded. "I guess you're right. I just wish I could have the excitement of New York City *and* the warmth of my family. That's really asking for too much, isn't it?"

"I don't know, Samantha. Did you ever consider that maybe you weren't meant to be a career woman? I think you have the ability to succeed if you put your mind to it, but I just wonder if you're willing to pay the price. Very few husbands enjoy being married to successful career women. A man likes his wife to be soft and comforting, not dynamic and competitive."

Yes, Samantha thought. A man wants a wife like Denise Gerard. Career girls are fine for a few hours' fun, but when it comes to marriage, a man wants a soft butterfly to soothe him after a hard day's work, to provide him with a home and children. Men try to have all that life can offer, fun with an accommodating secretary at the office and love in the gentle arms of a delicate wife, but a woman has to choose between love and a career. What did she care, though? The one man she really wanted was the one man she could never have. She shifted her thoughts from her own inner turmoil to force herself to consider Cory's problem. "How did they get the information for that story, Cory? Can't you sue them for invasion of privacy?"

"I don't think I have much of a case. It seems that I'm a well-known public figure and, as such, I must expect my life to be an open book, subject to invasion by any reporter who happens to be searching for an interesting topic to write about. In short, I have no privacy. I guess I shouldn't complain. I don't have half the problem that Jim Carson has. Say, he seems to be getting quite serious about your roommate. Is she prepared to deal with someone like Jim?"

"Oh," Samantha said, "Janet is a big girl. She can take care of herself."

Cory reflected for a minute before speaking. "And what about you, Samantha? Can you take care of yourself?" He shot an inquisitive glance in her direction.

Samantha felt strangely unnerved by Cory's searching gaze. She shifted restlessly toward the door, leaning away from his overpowering form. "Of course I can take care of myself. You, of all people, should realize my capabilities. Even Mrs. Harrison was impressed with my abilities before she became disillusioned by my appearance."

Cory's piercing eyes glinted down at her through half-closed lids. "I wasn't speaking of your secretarial skills; I was more concerned with you as a woman. Somehow I get the feeling that despite all your brave talk about being a liberated woman, you're still just a simple farm girl at heart."

Samantha bristled with suppressed anger. "Well, you can rearrange your thinking. Just because I'm not as sophisticated as Denise Gerard, don't get the impression that I'm a complete simpleton."

"Yes," Cory said. "We did decide that you were quite different from Denise, didn't we?" Then he became silent, apparently reflecting on the differences between Samantha and Denise.

Did he wish he had been able to bring the other girl with him instead? Samantha wondered. Inwardly she reproached herself for ever having agreed to accompany Cory at all. It might be all in the normal course of business for him, but she knew that she was too emotionally involved to maintain a business relationship twenty-four hours a day.

Cory had apparently torn himself away from his dreams of Denise and was talking about the passing scenery. "Have you ever been out to the Island before, Samantha?"

"No, I'm afraid I've spent most of my time exploring the city."

Cory laughed. "It's funny, country people can't wait to get to the city and city people yearn to live in the country. I guess it's the old story of wanting what we can't have."

How true, Samantha thought.

"In any case, I think you'll enjoy the Island.

It's quite different from upstate New York. The thing I love about it is your proximity to the water. There's a certain feeling that comes from looking at the unending expanse of the Atlantic Ocean and realizing that there's nothing to stop you until you reach Europe." He cast a tantalizing grin in her direction and his eyes traveled down her body in a manner so suggestive that she moved uncomfortably in her seat. Her discomfort only amused him more as he turned his eyes back to the road and murmured innocently, "There's a definite joy in exploring the treasures hidden beneath the depths of an icy surface." His good mood continued as he began to whistle softly to himself.

Samantha was infuriated. He seemed determined to continue baiting her. How could she ever conduct a civilized conversation with him so long as he regarded her as someone to be teased and toyed with? She stiffened her back and sat rigidly in her seat. Finally she closed her eyes, realizing that her best defense against him was to feign sleep. Even Cory Talbott couldn't argue with a sleeping person.

Samantha awoke slowly. A quick glance out the window showed that the traffic had thinned considerably and that the houses bordering the expressway were newer and spread farther apart than those they had passed earlier.

"Did you have a pleasant rest?" Cory asked. "You napped through the least interesting part of the trip. This area used to be all wooded except for an occasional potato farm, now it's a mass of housing tracts. All the beauty of the land has been destroyed. This blasted expressway keeps creeping farther and farther out on the Island, and each time it increases its length, more people scamper to buy the newly built houses. I certainly don't envy the husbands who spend hours sitting on this expressway just so their wives and kids can enjoy the delights of suburban life."

"I take it you wouldn't be willing to subject yourself to a long daily commute merely to assure your family of a more enjoyable life-style?"

Cory pursed his lips as if he were considering his answer very carefully. "It's hard to say. I really haven't given much thought to a family, let alone the life-style they would want. However, I can't imagine that my wife would be happy out here in a little development house, away from the excitement of the city, and I certainly can't see myself mowing the lawn and joining the local bowling league. No, I think my life would have to continue in the city and my wife would have to be able to meet the demands of a sophisticated life-style."

He shook his head incredulously. "How did we ever get onto this topic, anyway?" Disapproval was now clear in his tone. "I really can't see how my personal life can be of any interest to you. After all, we are just business acquaintances, aren't we?"

Samantha writhed under the piercing scrutiny of his mocking glare. "Yes, of course. I guess I was just trying to be polite to the boss."

"I understand," Cory said. "You wouldn't want me to place any significance on the topic we were discussing, right? I mean, you wouldn't be considering the possibility of sharing a cottage in suburbia with me, would you?" An amused glint flickered in his eyes.

"I should say not! We can't even take a short drive without fighting. There's absolutely no way a marriage between us could ever work out!"

Cory's entire face was beaming with the wicked grin curving from his mouth. "Who mentioned marriage? That relationship never entered the conversation, did it? I was merely investigating the possibility of us setting up housekeeping together. I'm quite surprised that a modern woman like you would even consider a binding relationship like marriage, at least without a tryout first. I always thought marriage was for more old-fashioned girls . . . the clinging-vine type, if you know what I mean."

Silence shrouded the car as Cory waited expectantly for an answer, and Samantha sank into sullen discomfort, wallowing in the misery of her own thoughts.

She could never admit to Cory that she *had* been considering what it would be like to be married to him, but much as she loved him, she was not the type to live with him under a housekeeping arrangement. That would be her final degradation; the ultimate revenge he could take for her little masquerade. To shame her by making her love him and then to show how little she really meant to him when he left her and married Denise Gerard.

Well, she wasn't about to let him do that to her.

She would never let him know that, much as she appeared to be independent on the outside, inside she was every bit as feminine as the fabulous Miss Gerard.

She was drawn out of her reveries by Cory's gently mocking voice. "Well, Samantha, you haven't answered me yet. What do you think about us setting up housekeeping together? We could probably get a nice little apartment near the World Trade Center and then I wouldn't have to travel uptown if I didn't feel like it. We'd be able to take our work home with us and get quite a bit accomplished. Then, of course, whenever the passion left the relationship, we'd both be free to go on to new and better things."

"And what would Denise think of this little arrangement? Wouldn't she object?"

"No problem," Cory said. "Denise knows I'm no angel. She doesn't expect me to toe the mark like some lovestruck schoolboy and she'd know that your relationship with me would be totally different from mine with her. So I don't think there's any problem with Denise. You know, the more we discuss this idea, the more intrigued I become with it. What do you say, Samantha? We're two normal, liberated adults. There's no reason we can't sustain a mature relationship. And you really are rather attractive, you know . . . in a very different way from Denise."

Samantha's anger was given new impetus by his unflattering comparison of her to Denise, and she forced herself to speak in a flippant manner she didn't really feel. "You may be able to hold me to my job with threats, but there's no way

you can ever force me to be anything more than
your secretary. I know you're a brilliant investor
and that I can learn more from working with
you than with anyone else, but I don't like you or
your kisses. So why do you think I would ever
want anything to do with you outside the office?"

Cory laughed. "You know, Samantha, I think
you're right. It would be sheer idiocy to ruin our
relationship by becoming romantically involved
with each other. You amuse me the way no other
woman ever has. I'd hate to see your razor-sharp
mind dulled by the sweet force of love."

"Don't worry," Samantha said. "You won't."
Her words sounded so brave; she only hoped
they were true. She hadn't been able to stop
herself from falling in love with Cory Talbott,
but she would do everything in her power to
prevent him from finding out. His callous
amusement would be more than she could bear.

During the course of their conversation the
scenery had changed again. The houses were
now larger and farther apart and the grounds
between them were heavily wooded. They
crossed a small bridge and Cory suddenly became more relaxed.

"I always feel better once we've left the high-
way. The expressway ends at the Hamptons and
from here on, it's a two-lane country road. It's
slower, but definitely more relaxed. I think the
journey over this road helps to prepare me for
the slow pace of Sag Harbor."

Samantha watched as they drove through the
small country towns. The houses seemed like
tiny New England cottages. Some were painted

white but many had a weatherbeaten gray look from years near the sea.

Cory turned the car off the main road in Sag Harbor onto a long paved driveway bearing a sign saying PRIVATE ROAD. The drive wound through a pine-filled, wooded area and along a sandy beach. At the crest of the beach stood a low, sprawling house entirely covered with hand-split cedar shingles. Cory drove into a carport jutting out from the lower level of the house. He took the luggage from the back of the car and went into the house, leaving Samantha to follow on her own. Terrance and Martha, the couple who kept house for him, were already there and Samantha could smell a savory aroma coming from the kitchen.

Cory sniffed the air. "Ah, Martha is cooking the cioppino already. Wait till you taste it. It's like nothing you've ever had before."

Cory passed the luggage to Terrance, then led Samantha to the library. Although the rest of the house might have the relaxed look of wicker furniture and salty summer breezes, the library was an extension of Cory's city office. Investment books lined the walls and an electronic ticker was set up at the side of the big walnut desk.

He settled himself behind the desk, removed some papers from his briefcase, told Samantha to get Mrs. Harrison on the telephone, then began punching out stocks on the machine, listing the prices as they flashed onto the screen. Samantha said a few inconsequential words to Mrs. Harrison and put Cory on the line immediately. He checked out some information with Mrs. Harrison and told her where he could be reached, instructing her to keep this information from everyone else.

Then his voice became agitated. "What can I do to get them off my back? . . . All right, if they think I'm engaged to Denise Gerard, don't deny it. Maybe they'll leave me alone if they think I'm spoken for." He slammed the receiver down and snorted angrily to himself.

Samantha's heart skipped a beat. Her worst fears had finally been confirmed. Cory had admitted that he was going to marry Denise. She bit her lip and turned away to hide the tears that had come suddenly to her eyes.

The rest of the day was much like any other day at the office might have been, and Samantha quite forgot where they were, though Cory's soon to be announced engagement was never far from her mind.

The cioppino Martha had made for dinner was everything Cory had promised it would be, with tasty bits of lobster, shrimp and filleted fish swimming in a spicy tomato sauce, and the crisp green salad and warm French bread were the perfect accompaniments.

Samantha leaned back after her coffee and placed her hands against her stomach. "I don't remember when I've enjoyed a meal so much. I feel so stuffed, I'll have to waddle up to bed."

Cory smiled and came over to her chair. "That's one of the things you don't know about beach living. After a filling dinner like that we take a refreshing stroll along the sand. Go get a sweater; the sea air can be chilly when the sun goes down."

When Samantha returned with her sweater, Cory was waiting for her at the front door, a windbreaker draped over one shoulder. He took Samantha's hand in his and led her toward the water after telling her to leave her shoes on the porch. Dusk was falling and the seashore had taken on a sleepy feeling which sent waves of lethargy undulating through Samantha's tired limbs.

Cory stopped and lowered himself to the sand near the water line, drawing Samantha down next to him. "This is my favorite time of day whenever I'm out here. I love to sit and watch the sun disappear behind the water. His arms had been draped loosely around his drawn up knees. Now he released his knees and put one arm around Samantha's shoulders, gently drawing her to him until her head rested easily against his chest. The movement was so fluid and natural that Samantha had no chance to protest and she enjoyed the serenity of the moment, relaxing in the comfort of Cory's tender touch and watching the ruby sun vanish into the sea.

When the sun had disappeared from view, Samantha shivered and turned to Cory, uncomfortably aware that her behavior now had contradicted everything she had told him earlier. She would have to be more careful. "I suppose we ought to be going in."

Cory gripped her shoulder as she attempted to rise. "Don't go yet . . . the best is yet to come. In a few minutes the stars will come out, then the moon. The moon reflected on the water is something really special. I wouldn't want you to miss it."

Samantha leaned back, relaxing against his chest once more and pushing her fears aside. Just as he had said, the stars came drifting gradually into the sky, as if someone were slowly switching on a series of twinkling candelabra. Then the moon rose like a radiant beacon, casting an aura of golden luminosity over the earth below. The effect was every bit as beautiful as Cory had promised it would be and Samantha turned to him, her eyes glistening with the wonder of the scene before her.

His eyes caught hers and he turned toward her, gently pressing her back on the sand.

Samantha opened her mouth to protest, but Cory's lips came down to meet hers, silencing any objection she might have made. He was gentle, tenderly teasing her submissive lips, and he stroked her hair as he pillowed her head against the softly shifting sands. His lips left hers and traveled to the lobe of her ear, gently kissing and nibbling at it. She felt his warm breath against her ear as he kissed the slender column of her neck and dropped his lips to the throbbing hollow just beneath it.

She moaned and twisted her head in the sand, not knowing what she wanted, and he heard her cries and brought his lips down on hers to silence any doubts she might feel. Then his hand began stroking her hip, traveling up along the side of her breast and coming to rest at the open vee of her neckline. He caressed her welcoming flesh as his hands began undoing the buttons of her blouse. His lips left hers as he whispered hoarsely, "I want you Samantha—and I mean to have you for my own."

His words came drifting through to Samantha as if in a dream. These weren't words of love. These were words of mere desire. Cory had never ever said that he loved her. She had no doubt that he desired her. The virile strength of his body against hers gave testimony to that. But she still had enough self-respect to prevent her yearning flesh from committing her to an action she would regret forever. She raised her hands against his chest and pushed him from her. "No, no, you promised you wouldn't force me. Let me go. . . . Please, I can't stand it."

Cory sat up and looked down at her. "I said I wouldn't force my attentions on you, Samantha; but I never said I wouldn't try to make you want my attentions, and you *did* want them just now, didn't you? Why are you fighting me?"

Samantha rose to her feet and screamed, in a nearly hysterical voice, "I'm not a toy you can use any way you want. I'm a human being, free to choose who I want to share my affections with, and I don't want to share them with you!" She ran into the house and upstairs, slamming the door to her room and locking it behind her.

She stood rigid, with her back pressed against the door, her heart beating a wild tattoo that seemed to reverberate through the silent room. Then she heard the outer door open and close, and Cory's footsteps padded toward her room. He tapped softly on the bolted door.

"Samantha, let me in. I want to talk to you."

Samantha felt as if a great weight were pressing against her chest. She could hardly summon enough breath to speak. "No, we have nothing to say to each other. Please go away."

There was an expectant silence as Samantha closed her eyes and balled her hands into tight fists. Then Cory's smoothly controlled voice came softly through the door. "All right, Samantha; we'll have our little talk in the morning. I hope you'll feel better after a good night's rest." He moved away from her door and she heard him enter his own room.

Samantha's composure left her completely and her body started to shake with tension. She covered her face with her hands and walked to the window.

As the stealthy gray fingers of dawn came creeping through the window, she took her small valise and went quietly out of the house, walking back to town to catch the bus and start the long trip back to the city.

Chapter Nine

The towering oak trees shivered in the heavy October breeze, shedding their leafy burden bit by bit. Indian summer was a colorful season in upstate New York, an unexpected bonus of delightfully warm weather before the onslaught of winter storms.

Samantha sat by the lake, her velvety blond hair drawn back from her face with a blue satin ribbon that matched her eyes. Her back rested against the sturdy trunk of a fat oak tree and she nibbled lazily on a blade of dry grass while staring at the placid waters. Everything was so peaceful and quiet in this wooded glen that it was hard to imagine the turmoil that had filled her life a few short weeks ago.

She had finally decided that the double strain placed upon her by Cory's desire both for vengeance and for her was too great to bear and, after leaving the beach house in Sag Harbor, she had returned to Greenwich Village, packed her things and caught the next bus home. Janet tried to get an explanation from her, but Samantha would volunteer nothing. She gave Janet her share of the next two months' rent and promised to return soon, though privately she doubted she would ever go back.

Janet had watched as Samantha wrote a letter of resignation, mailed it, and immediately began filling suitcases with her clothing. Cory phoned, but Samantha refused to speak with him, and before he had a chance to drive in from Sag Harbor she was on her way to the small upstate town where her parents lived.

As she sat here, relaxing in the clean, fresh country air, she saw no need ever to return to the city. Her parents were delighted to have her back; they had never liked the idea of her living in New York City. Now they saw the possibility of her marrying within their community and settling on a nearby farm. The prospect of Samantha's living close by, with a flock of grandchildren for them to enjoy in their golden years, was a thought that brought them endless joy.

She had been hired by the local bank, and even old Mr. Hardings, the manager, was impressed with her financial acumen. Ken Hardings, his son, was definitely showing more than a passing interest in her and she knew that a little encouragement on her part would lead to a proposal. But she could never marry Ken. He never set her heart racing the way Cory Talbott had, even though she knew Cory only thought of her as a desirable woman to be conquered and thrown aside when his revenge was complete.

In any case, there was no point in thinking about returning to the city, since she was sure that Cory had remained steadfast in his determination to ruin any chances she might have for getting another job. Maybe he had been right about her; maybe she wasn't meant to be a career woman.

The gentle rustling of the fallen leaves behind her indicated movement in the forest. Samantha looked up, expecting to see a fawn or squirrel or some other of the various woodland denizens; instead she saw a face she had never thought to see again. Cory Talbott was staring down at her.

Her voice rang out in an angry, startled explosion. "You . . . what are you doing here? This is private property. I'm not your employee now and I don't have to endure your company anymore." She started to stand, but Cory's muscular hands pushed her back to the ground.

"Sit down!" he snarled. "You're just as impossible as you always were. I'm not going to bite you. If you could ever bother to behave in a polite, civilized manner maybe we wouldn't always end up arguing." He lowered himself to the ground and sat beside her.

Samantha was unrepentant. "There's no need for me to be polite to you. I don't want anything further to do with you. Thanks to you I've left New York and my dreams of a career and resumed my life in the country. Don't you think you've punished me enough? I'm warning you, there's not much more you can do to me, so you might as well consider the matter closed."

"My thoughts exactly, Samantha. I've decided to forgive you for your little escapade and I'm here to accept your apology."

Samantha bounded to her feet and stood glaring down at him. "You want *me* to apologize? What nerve. I admit what I did was wrong, but I apologized for it a long time ago. You're the one who blew everything all out of proportion until you convined yourself to engage in a personal vendetta against me. Then, once you completely ruined any chance I might have had for a career, you followed me here and now you expect me to apologize to you *again!* My apology will come when Satan plays with snowballs!"

Cory grabbed her hand and pulled her back down beside him. "Oh, stop it, Samantha. I swear you have such a flair for the dramatic that you should have been the actress instead of Janet. I didn't follow you here. If you'd stop wallowing in your own misery long enough you'd realize that the U.S. Grand Prix just took place in Watkins Glen. I told you I was a racing enthusiast. Then I spent ten days at Cornell University, presenting a seminar on the economics of the stock market. So you see, I spent the last two weeks in upstate New York—on business. That's why I'm here, not to inflict some mortal punishment on you. Janet heard I would be in the area and asked me to stop by and see how you were. Your mother told me you were out walking in the woods. *Now* do you think we could have a normal conversation?"

Samantha's head was spinning. Cory had come in a spirit of friendliness and at Janet's request. She realized how childish her actions must seem to him. After all, he had no idea of the turmoil her love for him was creating inside of her. "I'm sorry, Cory. It was nice of you to come. It's just that we've been fighting so much I can't imagine us having a civil relationship. How is Janet? I haven't heard from her for a while."

"I know. That's one of the reasons she asked me to stop by and see you. Janet and Jim have gotten pretty serious about each other. I wouldn't be surprised if they started discussing marriage soon. In that case, Janet would have to give up the apartment, unless you wanted her to keep it for you."

Samantha wasn't surprised to hear about Janet and Jim. She had noticed how close they were becoming before she left New York. "I guess you were wrong about Jim, then. He must not be the Lothario you made him out to be."

Cory shook his head. "I wouldn't say that. Let's just say that Janet was woman enough to tame him."

Samantha smiled sadly. "I'm happy for Janet. I know she really loves Jim, and I know they're going to be happy together. No matter what you say, I think they're two of the best people I know."

Cory considered carefully before speaking. "You may be right, but lately they haven't been very nice to me. In addition to having me find out how you were, Janet wanted me to tell you that I wouldn't hinder you in your job hunting if you should decide to return to New York. She explained the entire situation to me and maybe I have been too harsh on you. You can even have your job back if you want, and I promise not to badger you anymore."

Samantha stood up and glowered down at Cory. "Just like that! You disrupt my entire life, send me running back to my parents, and then, just because one of your clients tells you that maybe you were being too harsh on me, you come up here and expect me to come running back! Well, forget it! This may not be Wall Street, but at least people around here respect me."

Cory stood up and grasped Samantha's upper arms roughly. "You're still the same old spitfire, aren't you? You haven't heard a word I've said, have you? I did *not* come up here to apologize! And *nobody* makes me do something I don't want to do, not my clients or anyone else. There isn't enough money in the world to force me to do something against my will. I was trying to be nice to you, something your conniving little brain is apparently unable to comprehend. I don't know how I can ever get through to you. You're the most impossible woman I've ever met."

Samantha challenged his stormy gray eyes. "Why bother trying to get through to me? Why don't you just forget me and leave me alone?"

Cory drew her to him, bruising her arms with

his violence, his steel-strong arms imprisoning
her against him. His sharp eyes still flashed like
icy diamonds but a gentle softness hovered in
the background as if it were too uncertain to risk
emergence.

His voice was husky and uneven when he
spoke. "I wish to hell I could leave you alone.
But you haunt my days and nights like some
pagan witch. I want you when we're apart, and
when we're together I can't keep my hands off
you. There's nowhere you can run that I won't
find you." His mouth came down roughly on
hers, branding her with his kiss and becoming
an instrument of exquisite torture. His fingers
moved lower on her back, gently caressing every
inch of her flaming skin.

Samantha's nerves were strained to the
breaking point. Her hands involuntarily left her
sides and captured his head, pressing it closer
and increasing the firmness of his lips upon hers
until her mind was totally inoperative and only
primitive emotions dictated her actions.

Cory's lips gentled when he felt Samantha's
impassioned response. He pressed her head
back and lowered his lips to her ear, caressing it
with his gentle kisses and warm, moist breath.
His insistent lips traveled to the arch of her
neck, covering the gently pulsing vein with
short, intimate kisses and moving ever farther
downward to find the soft hollow between her
breasts, where he seemed to breath so deeply
that Samantha felt he was actually inhaling the
deep love that was exploding in her heart.

Gently, he braced her with his hands and

urged her down until she rested on the soft bed of leaves beneath the huge oak tree. He shifted his weight above her and began stroking her hair. "I want you, Samantha. It's senseless to go on fighting what we both feel."

Samantha saw the torrid desire raging in his eyes and the simmering passion born of love froze in her heart. Just desire for her, that was all he had ever felt. Never once had he expressed any love for her, just desire. He had come after her to take what he wanted and put his erotic yearnings at an end. Once he had quenched his body's need for her, he would be free to wed Denise, treating her with all the love and respect a man reserved for the woman he married.

The thought of Cory making love to her, then leaving her still burning for his touch while he ran back to Denise's waiting arms sent an icy chill racing through Samantha's veins. She twisted beneath him, kicking and pummeling his chest in her desire to be free. The sudden violence of her reaction caught him completely unaware and she was suddenly free, getting to her feet and looking down at him while he gazed at her in complete confusion, unrequited desire still blazing in his startled eyes.

Fear of his power over her and disgust at the eager response of her own body drove Samantha's fury. "I hate you. You're just like all the others. I won't be your plaything. I'm a human being, not a plastic doll. Now get back to your racing cars and business machines or whatever other toys you can find to amuse yourself with and leave me alone! I don't ever want to see you again! You disgust me, Cory Talbott!" She turned and ran from him, the tears streaming down her face as she raced toward home.

Samantha reached the house and ran past her mother, who asked if she had seen the young man from New York who had come by to see her. She nodded and ran into her room, closing the door behind her. Her breath came in short gasps; she was winded from running and her heart was pounding.

The tears were drying on her cheeks when she heard the sound of a car motor starting up. She ran to the window and saw Cory's Jaguar speed away. A deep void in her heart wanted him back . . . wanted to feel his caresses on any terms . . . but her head told her it was better this way.

The next few weeks went by uneventfully. Samantha continued to impress the people at the bank with her financial knowledge, and Mr. Hardings seemed extremely pleased to see Ken's developing interest in her. He did all he could to encourage the relationship, but Samantha's emotions were frozen. Cory Talbott might not have had what he wanted from her body, but he had certainly stolen her heart.

Janet's play had opened to rave reviews in Boston and Philadelphia and she was hailed by the critics as a promising new star on the Broadway horizon. Samantha's delight for Janet was

compounded when she received a short but
happy note inviting her to attend Janet's wedding to Jim two weeks before their show opened
on Broadway.

She received the invitation with mixed emotions. There was no doubting her happiness for
Janet and Jim. Her mixed emotions came from
the knowledge that Cory Talbott was sure to be
at the wedding—probably with Denise Gerard.
But she decided that her relationship with Janet
was much too important to be ruined by Cory
Talbott. He had already created enough havoc in
her life; she was not going to allow him to
deprive her of the pleasure of seeing Janet married.

Samantha drove down to New York. She hated
to drive in the city, but it seemed to be the best
way to travel since she was loaded down with
Janet's wedding present and all her own clothes.
It was a four-and-a-half-hour trip to the city and
she wore comfortable jeans and a tee shirt for
the tedious journey. A warm white parka completed her outfit.

Janet had taken a room at the hotel where she
and Jim were being married, so Samantha had
the Greenwich Village apartment to herself
when she arrived. Luckily, there had been no
traffic and she had completed the trip in plenty
of time to have a relaxing bath before she
dressed. Her dress was one she had bought on
impulse one day when she was out with Janet,
and it was far more expensive than anything she
had ever bought before or since. In fact, she
would never have even considered it if Janet

hadn't been so insistent. So it seemed only right that she should wear it to Janet's wedding.

Actually, the dress was very plain. It was made of supple black silk and its wide shoulder straps curved down to a simple rounded neck, then it nipped in slightly at the waist before falling to her ankles in a smooth fluid line. The dress had no personality of its own and only came to life when it molded itself to Samantha's curvaceous body. Then it took on a strangely sensuous appearance as if it had been made for Samantha alone.

As she looked in the mirror, Samantha had to thank Janet for her insistence; the dress made her look sophisticated, almost like one of the glamorous actresses with whom Janet associated. High-heeled black sandals showed off her legs through the long slit at the side of the dress. A simple gold chain around her neck and a bangle bracelet on her arm were the only jewelry she wore. Her shiny flaxen hair hung loosely to her shoulders and her face glowed with a radiance more natural than artificial.

She slipped into her velvet cape and walked downstairs to meet the taxi she had called.

The reception room was crowded with guests, and Samantha pressed through the crowd, trying to find Janet and Jim. Finally she saw Janet standing in the middle of a large group of people. When Janet spotted Samantha, she rushed over and hugged her effusively.

"Oh, Sam, I'm so glad to see you. I've missed you so much."

"Yes," boomed a loud masculine voice. "She's been so lonely that she's decided to take a new roommate."

Samantha looked up to see Jim grinning down at her as he slipped behind Janet and placed his hand possessively on her slender waist. "Who is this ravishing creature returned from the wild? Could it be that you've kept her hidden away from me lest I change my mind about becoming a solid, married citizen?"

Janet poked Jim playfully in the ribs. "Cut it out, Jim. I made Samantha buy that dress, but I could never get her to wear it before, so I take it as a special compliment that she's chosen to wear it tonight. Don't make her nervous or she'll be mad at me for making her buy it."

"Very well, my dear. Far be it from me to argue with my bride-to-be on our wedding night. In truth, Samantha, you look thoroughly ravishing. But, alas, my romantic life is no longer my own. I am spoken for. So I'll have to find someone else to put some masculine spice into your life."

"That's O.K., Jim; I'll be fine on my own. I do know a few people here, you know."

Samantha was deep in conversation with Janet's mother when she glanced across the room and saw Cory Talbott.

His strong brown fingers stroked the edges of his highball glass as he casually lounged against the fireplace, his dark, hand-tailored evening suit accenting the masculine power which surged beneath it. Samantha marveled at the effect his presence had upon her. If only he had smiled, she would have walked into his arms willingly, begging him to forgive her and accept her love. But his eyes only raked her body disapprovingly before he turned to listen to the man next to him.

Samantha was surprised that Denise wasn't with him. Why would Cory be unaccompanied this evening? Maybe Denise was talking to someone else? But a careful scan of the room revealed no sign of her. Samantha had no idea what to think as she moved with the others into the room where the ceremony would be held.

Cory's eyes followed her all through the ceremony and at the reception afterward. His face was frozen in a permanent scowl, and each time Samantha felt his icy, gray gaze resting on her she became more convinced that he would never stop despising her.

She realized now that love was more important to her than any career, and the only love she wanted was Cory's. But he hated her and was going to marry Denise, so she would have to content herself with the cold comfort of a career in her small hometown.

Janet and Jim said their farewells and left for a secluded honeymoon weekend at Jim's Ozark retreat. Samantha was trying to fend off the advances of a guest who had had slightly too much to drink when a familiar voice sounded beside her.

"That's O.K., Jeffers, I'll take care of Samantha now."

The man tightened his grip on Samantha's wrist. "Forget it, Talbott. This one is mine. Find your own pillow pal for tonight."

Before anyone knew what had happened, Cory lunged for the man, who backed off, knocking Samantha to the floor, where she hit her head against the leg of a small French chair.

Samantha protested weakly when Cory bent and lifted her in his arms. Her head still throbbed with the pain of her fall. "You don't have to take care of me. I don't work for you anymore. Just leave me alone."

Cory shrugged off her objections. "You're in no condition to know what you're doing. I don't know what's gotten into you, Samantha. First you come here dressed like Mata Hari and then you start hanging around with that creep. Do you have any idea what would have happened if I had left you with him?"

"Nothing would have happened! I'm perfectly able to take care of myself. You're always trying to believe the worst of me. You just can't stand the thought that another man might find me as desirable as you find Denise."

"Leave Denise out of this," Cory said as he handed the doorman his parking ticket.

The parking attendant brought Cory's car and Cory deposited Samantha on the seat where the pain and the champagne she had drunk soon sent her escaping into sleep.

When she awoke the next morning her head felt as if it were a huge balloon about to burst and her mouth tasted sour and cottony. The slender strip of sunlight streaming through the window made her wince in pain and she turned her face away. Slowly, she came fully awake and realized that she wasn't in her own room in the Village. This room was definitely masculine in tone. Deep brown carpeting covered the floor, and the walls were covered with a heavy beige grasscloth. Starkly simple furniture filled the room, and dark bamboo blinds shielded the windows.

Slowly the events of the past evening came drifting into her mind. She remembered getting into Cory's car, but nothing after that. What on earth was she doing here?

Her evening dress and cape lay on a nearby chair and she was dressed only in her brief bikini undergarments. She shivered with embarrassment and lifted her head from the pillow. She was immediately attacked by the blinding flash of a headache, which forced her back against the pillow. She knew she had to leave this room, but she was entirely too sick to move. Moaning painfully, she closed her eyes and cradled her head deeper into the pillow.

The door creaked slowly open and soft footsteps padded across the room, coming to a halt beside the bed. Samantha half opened one eye to see who was standing beside the bed. One quick glance at the familiar masculine figure and her startled eyes flew open to look directly into the troubled eyes of Cory Talbott. He smiled dryly down at her.

"I see you've rejoined the world of the living. How are you feeling?"

Samantha closed her eyes and groaned. "Terrible."

Cory shook his head in disgust. "I'm not surprised, considering the size of the bump on your head. But don't worry, the doctor said it's nothing that a few hours of rest won't cure. He came to see you last night, you know, but you didn't even wake up."

"I think I'm dying."

Cory laughed. "Well, you can be thankful that, bad as it seems, the condition isn't fatal and you'll probably be fully recovered by tomorrow. For the present, the only thing you can do is close your eyes and rest up. You blacked out in the car, so I took you to my apartment, called the doctor, and put you to bed. I didn't think you'd want to ruin your siren outfit by sleeping in it, so I removed it."

"Do you mean to say that you undressed me last night?"

Cory made a wry face. "Come off it, Samantha. It's not the first time I've seen a woman in her underwear, and, I might add, I'm quite familiar with even more intimate parts of the female anatomy. So your frilly undergarments held no erotic surprises for me. Rest assured that your virtue is still intact. Now go to sleep; you're in no condition to discuss anything. I'll talk to you later, when you're feeling better."

He left the room, closing the door softly behind him, and Samantha drifted off into a troubled sleep. When she awoke, the sultry shadows of a lazy summer evening were enveloping the room.

She opened her eyes slowly and familiarized herself with her surroundings. Her inquisitive gaze drifted to the chair where her discarded clothing had been and met the softly studious eyes of Cory Talbott.

"You've slept the day away. How are you feeling now?"

Samantha moved her head from side to side and raised it off the pillow, pulling the sheet around her shoulders as she sat up. "I feel fine now." She paused, then added reluctantly, "Thanks for taking care of me. I don't want to impose on you anymore, though. If you'll get me my clothes and leave the room I'll get dressed and go home."

Cory shook his head as he walked slowly to the bed, his eyes flowing possessively over her body. He wore black silk pajama bottoms and his chest was bare. Samantha's heart did a somersault and began racing so wildly that she could hardly hear his voice over the loud tattoo.

"Not right now. It will be dark soon, and I scarcely think it wise for you to be wandering around Manhattan in that seductive outfit of yours. You can spend the night here and I'll take you home in the morning . . . if you still want me to," he said, flashing his arrogant, mocking smile.

Samantha felt extremely vulnerable, and her trembling fingers held the sheet tightly beneath her chin. She looked up at him entreatingly. "Please, Cory. Let me go home. I don't want to fight with you anymore."

Cory lowered himself to the bed and placed his hand beneath her chin, raising it so their eyes met. "Then *don't* fight me anymore. That's all I ever wanted, you know. I just wanted you to stop fighting me and start loving me." He slipped beneath the covers and cradled Samantha's soft body against the hardness of his own.

She rolled away from him. "Don't touch me. Please, don't touch me."

He reached out and turned her onto her back. "You're asking the impossible. I couldn't keep my hands off you even if I wanted to." As if to prove his statement, his fingers caressed her cheek and moved slowly down her neck, tracing a light path across the curve of her breast.

"Cory . . ." Samantha's voice was a plea, but she wasn't sure if she wanted him to stop or to continue.

Cory had no such problem. He knew exactly what he wanted, and his mouth closed over Samantha's, firmly overruling any objections her mind was raising. His hand glided behind her back, releasing the clasp of her bra, and she felt his rough chest pressing against her now naked breasts.

The shock of her nudity brought her back to sanity once more and she raised her palms, pushing him away from her. He moved back, but his eyes drifted from her face and settled on her body. His hands followed his gaze, tenderly caressing, tantalizing her nipples into peaks of erotic passion, and she began to sob quietly, her body shaking with the force of her emotions. His gentle expression turned to one of utter bewilderment. "Now what's wrong? Am I never going to understand you, Samantha?"

"You've taken everything—my career, my pride, my love. You've left me nothing—not even my body."

Cory smiled, but his voice was low and husky. His lips traveled where his hands had been, and Samantha moaned softly.

"You're right, my love. I want everything. I want to know every inch of you." Lifting her chin with his thumbs, he caught her head between his hands. "Your mind as well as your body. No secrets—no disguises—nothing between us but skin and flesh." His fingers slipped down to the flimsy elastic of her one remaining garment.

Samantha reached out to stop him. "Cory, don't do this." She twisted away from him and buried her head in the pillow. "I want to go home, Cory. I can't stay . . . not now . . . I love you too much . . . too much to know your love for one evening and then watch you walk away to Denise's arms."

Cory gripped her shoulders, raising her to face him. "Is that what you think, you little fool? Do you think I would invest so much time in you if I only wanted to have an affair with you? Don't you know that you've had me under your spell from the first moment I looked into your eyes when you came barreling down Wall Street?" He smiled at her shocked look. "Those blue eyes made an indelible impression on me. Even that terrible disguise couldn't keep me from wanting you. I thought I was losing my mind, wanting to make love to a woman who dressed like a drill sergeant. Thank heaven for the blackout. When I saw you at your apartment, I realized I had found the woman I couldn't forget, but you were so angry—so determined to fight me. I couldn't let you get away—that's why I threatened you. I had to keep you near me any way I could."

His hand combed through her hair, curving it softly over her shoulders. "I want to marry you . . . if you don't mind giving up your status as a liberated woman. It's only fair—I haven't been a free man since the day I met you."

Samantha looked stunned. "Marry me? But you told the magazine you were going to marry Denise."

Cory chuckled. "Denise is a frivolous society girl. Ours was a relationship of convenience. I haven't seen her since I took her out that night and found myself thinking of you. If you remember, I came back to the office to get you. I never told her I loved her, and I never asked her to marry me. I only told the magazine I was engaged to her because it seemed to be the simplest way to get those other crazy women off my back, and I never told you I loved you because I was afraid of frightening you off. Everytime I went near you you jumped at my touch. But I'm not afraid anymore. Did you know that you talk in your sleep? So I have reason to believe that your little act is finally over and I've discovered the true Samantha, the one who'll be my wife, the mother to my children, and grow old beside me. I love you, Samantha, and I want you to marry me. Do you think you could be happy with a career as my wife?"

Samantha threw herself into Cory's arms and buried her head in his chest. "Oh yes, Cory, a million times, yes! I guess I've loved you . . . from the first moment I saw you, but I had on that horrid disguise. Then afterwards, you were so angry, I thought you would never forgive me, and when Denise told me that you were in love with her, I thought everything was hopeless."

Cory lifted her head gently. "I'm hopelessly in love with you, and the only way I can survive is by having you by my side . . . holding you in my arms . . . kissing those sweet lips. But right now, I think you'd better get out of bed so we can drive up to your parents' home. I don't trust myself to be alone with you now that I know you love me as much I love you, and I don't intend to spoil my honorable intentions toward you."

Samantha smiled smugly and lay back against the pillows, twining her arms around Cory's neck and pulling him down with her. "It's a long trip up to the farm, and I don't like driving at night. Besides, I don't think I'm ready to get out of bed yet. In fact, I don't feel well enough to be left alone. You'd better stay here with me."

Cory framed her face with his hands. "Do you know what you're saying, Samantha? Do you trust me that much?"

"I trust you with my life—my love—everything. Nothing held back, nothing between us but skin and flesh—remember? We can do the paperwork on Monday, but for now I want you here beside me."

Cory's lips nuzzled the arch of her neck. "Anything you say, my love—but I can't promise that you'll get much rest." His lips moved onto hers, and the time for talking was over.

Silhouette Romance

IT'S YOUR OWN SPECIAL TIME

Contemporary romances for today's women.
Each month, six very special love stories will be yours
from SILHOUETTE. Look for them wherever books are sold
or order now from the coupon below.

$1.50 each

___#61 WHISPER MY NAME Michaels	___#80 WONDER AND WILD DESIRE Stephens
___#62 STAND-IN BRIDE Halston	___#81 IRISH THOROUGHBRED Roberts
___#63 SNOWFLAKES IN THE SUN Brent	___#82 THE HOSTAGE BRIDE Dailey
___#64 SHADOW OF APOLLO Hampson	___#83 LOVE LEGACY Halston
___#65 A TOUCH OF MAGIC Hunter	___#84 VEIL OF GOLD Vitek
___#66 PROMISES FROM THE PAST Vitek	___#85 OUTBACK SUMMER John
___#67 ISLAND CONQUEST Hastings	___#86 THE MOTH AND THE FLAME Adams
___#68 THE MARRIAGE BARGAIN Scott	___#87 BEYOND TOMORROW Michaels
___#69 WEST OF THE MOON St. George	___#88 AND THEN CAME DAWN Stanford
___#70 MADE FOR EACH OTHER Afton Bonds	___#89 A PASSIONATE BUSINESS James
___#71 A SECOND CHANCE ON LOVE Ripy	___#90 WILD LADY Major
___#72 ANGRY LOVER Beckman	___#91 WRITTEN IN THE STARS Hunter
___#73 WREN OF PARADISE Browning	___#92 DESERT DEVIL McKay
___#74 WINTER DREAMS Trent	___#93 EAST OF TODAY Browning
___#75 DIVIDE THE WIND Carroll	___#94 ENCHANTMENT Hampson
___#76 BURNING MEMORIES Hardy	___#95 FOURTEEN KARAT BEAUTY Wisdom
___#77 SECRET MARRIAGE Cork	___#96 LOVE'S TREACHEROUS JOURNEY Beckman
___#78 DOUBLE OR NOTHING Oliver	___#97 WANDERER'S DREAM Clay
___#79 TO START AGAIN Halldorson	___#98 MIDNIGHT WINE St. George
	___#99 TO HAVE, TO HOLD Camp

$1.75 each

___# 100 YESTERDAY'S SHADOW Stanford	___# 106 THE LANCASTER MEN Dailey
___# 101 PLAYING WITH FIRE Hardy	___# 107 TEARS OF MORNING Bright
___# 102 WINNER TAKE ALL Hastings	___# 108 FASCINATION Hampson
___# 103 BY HONOUR BOUND Cork	___# 112 WHISPER WIND Stanford
___# 104 WHERE THE HEART IS Vitek	___# 113 WINTER BLOSSOM Browning
___# 105 MISTAKEN IDENTITY Eden	___# 114 PAINT ME RAINBOWS Michaels
___# 109 FIRE UNDER SNOW Vernon	___# 115 A MAN FOR ALWAYS John
___# 110 A STRANGER'S WIFE Trent	___# 116 AGAINST THE WIND Lindley
___# 111 WAYWARD LOVER South	___# 117 MANHATTAN MASQUERADE Scott

- - - - - - - - - - - - - - - -

SILHOUETTE BOOKS, Department SB/1
1230 Avenue of the Americas
New York, NY 10020

Please send me the books I have checked above. I am enclosing
$_____ (please add 50¢ to cover postage and handling. NYS and
NYC residents please add appropriate sales tax). Send check or
money order—no cash or C.O.D.'s please. Allow six weeks for delivery.

NAME_____

ADDRESS_____

CITY_____STATE/ZIP_____

Silhouette ❤ *Romance*

15-Day Free Trial Offer
6 Silhouette Romances

6 Silhouette Romances, free for 15 days! We'll send you 6 new Silhouette Romances to keep for 15 days, absolutely free! If you decide not to keep them, send them back to us. You pay nothing.

Free Home Delivery. But if you enjoy them as much as we think you will, keep them by paying the invoice enclosed with your free trial shipment. We'll pay all shipping and handling charges. You get the convenience of Home Delivery and we pay the postage and handling charge each month.

Don't miss a copy. The Silhouette Book Club is the way to make sure you'll be able to receive every new romance we publish before they're sold out. There is no minimum number of books to buy and you can cancel at any time.

This offer expires April 30, 1982

Silhouette Book Club, Dept. **SBI**17B
120 Brighton Road, Clifton, NJ 07012

   Please send me 6 Silhouette Romances to keep for 15 days, absolutely free. I understand I am not obligated to join the Silhouette Book Club unless I decide to keep them.

NAME_____

ADDRESS_____

CITY_____ STATE_____ ZIP_____